'Murray Watts is a master s
lots of them. Expect twists
traditions and an awkward look
afterwards. Spellbinding.'
Paul Kerensa, comedian and author

'Brilliantly written . . . Murray Watts is a master of words and has a unique and wonderful insight into the meaning of the Bible and putting it into stories. Through this short but beautifully crafted book, you will be entertained, educated and inspired to think, and your heart and faith will be enriched as a result.'
Rosemary Conley, CBE, DL

Murray Watts began his career writing and performing stories for BBC Radio Merseyside in 1971. He studied English literature and the history of art at Emmanuel College, Cambridge, where he began writing plays. In 1975, he joined Upstream Theatre in London, founded by Richard Everett, as resident writer and associate director. He continued to work for Upstream for many years but, in 1977, he joined Paul Burbridge and Nigel Forde as co-founders of Riding Lights Theatre Company in York. He wrote and directed many shows for the company before leaving to join BBC Wales as an associate producer and broadcaster in 1987. Since then, Murray has written many plays for theatre and radio and numerous screenplays for TV and film. His award-winning play, *The Fatherland*, inspired by his theatre work in Soweto, South Africa, was produced by Bush Theatre at Riverside Studios in London in 1989 and, in 2012, a season of his plays was presented at the King's Head Theatre in London. He is perhaps best known as the screenwriter of the film *The Miracle Maker* and as the writer and director of the play *Mr Darwin's Tree*. Murray has also written many books since co-writing *Time to Act* with Paul Burbridge in 1978. He is the author of the bestselling *Lion Bible for Children*, now published in more than twenty languages. Twenty-five years ago, he moved to Scotland, where he founded the Wayfarer Trust, an arts charity based at Freswick Castle in Caithness, which provides encouragement and spiritual inspiration to many artists around the world.

YOURS TRULY

Parables and stories

Murray Watts

First published in Great Britain in 2019

Society for Promoting Christian Knowledge
36 Causton Street
London SW1P 4ST
www.spck.org.uk

British Library Cataloguing-in-Publication Data
A catalogue record for this book is available from the British Library

ISBN 978–0–281–08094–6
eBook ISBN 978–0–281–08095–3

Typeset by Falcon Oast Graphic Art Ltd
First printed in Great Britain by Ashford Colour Press
Subsequently digitally reprinted in Great Britain

eBook by Falcon Oast Graphic Art Ltd

Produced on paper from sustainable forests

For
Jock Stein
and
Oliver Vellacott,
with gratitude for years of
friendship, encouragement and love

Contents

Acknowledgements

I would like to thank Tony Collins, who has been my editor, working on many books with me, for more than forty years. He has been a loyal friend, encourager and inspirer. It was Tony and the team at SPCK who persuaded me to take a handful of these stories, add to them and create *Yours Truly*. I did not expect to write this book and I am grateful that the wisdom and insight of others have gently but insistently nudged me into sharing some of the parables and stories in my archive and my heart.

I would also like to thank Paul Burbridge and Nigel Forde, my dearest friends and co-founders of Riding Lights Theatre Company. Without their brilliant humour and invention and perseverance over the years, and their positive influence on my life, I doubt if any of these stories would have been created.

My thanks go also to the supporters and trustees of the Wayfarer Trust, the arts charity that has been so central to my life over the past twenty years. The Revd Jock Stein, chairman, is mentioned in my dedication but alongside him, as he has offered his untiring service to the trust, have been trustees Geoffrey Stevenson (and former trustee Judith Stevenson), Luke Walton, Susan Masterton, Nicole Smyth, Simon West and, once again, Paul Burbridge. They have all been great friends, counsellors and advisers, helping me and many artists to keep going, frequently against the odds. My special thanks also to artist Monique Sliedrecht, creative director of the Wayfarer Trust, for the friendship, inspiration and support she has given to myself and many fellow artists through her work for the trust and at Freswick Castle over many years. My thanks too to a former trustee, Helen Davies, my aunt, who celebrates her ninetieth birthday this year and has been a lifelong spiritual guide, mentor and personification of the love of God to me. Writing plays and telling stories was not an expected career for me and I needed visionary relatives and friends, as well as my long-suffering parents, to support me and to believe in me. Thank you to Martin and Colleen Barlow too, for their love and encouragement in recent years.

My gratitude also goes to actor Andrew Harrison, who has memorably performed in plays of mine over the years and has already brought some of these stories to the stage. By the time this book is published, he will be performing a one-man version of *Yours Truly* around the UK – a show fittingly premiered at the Greenbelt Festival 2019. It is not only his brilliance and great sense of humour that have given so much to me; it is also his loyal friendship.

Above all, thank you to my sons, Fionn and Toby Watts, young film-makers who have wonderfully failed to 'get a proper job' and are showing all the courage and risk-taking qualities that are required to survive and flourish in the arts world with all its desperate ups and downs. I was able to develop my story-telling skills with them, when they were little, and now they are telling stories of their own. Their faith, their hope and their humour have made me proud and given me courage to keep going and to keep dreaming.

Note on performing rights

Please note the following regarding reading and performing this material in public.

In all cases of public reading for non-paying audiences, in churches, schools and other contexts, please always state the title of the story, the book and the author, such as '"A Little Girl's Letter to God" from the book *Yours Truly*, written by Murray Watts (SPCK, 2019)'.

All enquiries about public reading, stage performance in a professional context, publication or broadcast, should be addressed to the publishers.

Introduction

I have worked in theatre, TV and film for many years so have encountered a few celebrities in my time. I wrote the piece *A Celebrity Questions Jesus* for an arts conference at Schloss Mittersill in Austria. It was used as part of a discussion about fame and trying to keep our lives balanced and sane, whether at the lowest or the highest levels of media exposure. The tragedy of the 'rich young ruler' mentioned in the Gospels continues to have a profound relevance to our own age.

Over the years, I have written quite a large number of stories for different contexts and the second story, *An Artist Tries to Create the World*, was written for La Fonderie, a group of French artists who had gathered in the Pavé d'Orsay gallery in Paris to consider the life of the artist. One of my themes was the perils of perfectionism. I have often been moved by the account of the creation in Genesis, which does not say that the world was perfect, but that 'God saw that it was good'.

The stories in this book often began with an 'itch' or an 'irritation', as a storyteller can be like a hapless oyster, producing something precious from an annoying grain of sand. *The Christmas Letter* began like that. After years of receiving many of these well-meaning round robin missives, I was finally compelled to write this.

This book began its life at the Greenbelt Festival in the early 1980s, when I first decided to write a parable to illustrate a talk. The talk, about Christianity and culture, has been long forgotten, but the parable, *The Village Secret*, survives.

Ten of the stories in *Yours Truly* were written specially for the book in recent times and *The Plague* is one of these. It began, however, as a thought that had been lurking in my mind since the late 1980s, when there was so much judge-mentalism regarding the HIV and AIDS crisis.

New headteachers, inspirational CEOs, visionary church leaders, all face familiar resistance. I remember a story told by Richard Hare, former bishop of Pontefract, about a visit to a parish church in Yorkshire. The verger had been there for forty years and the bishop said to him, 'You must have seen many changes in your time.' 'Yes,' the verger replied, 'and I have opposed every single one of them.' *The Greatest Discovery in the World* is a dark little reflection on that perennial sub-ject – the threat of change to the status quo.

In 2009, I was commissioned to write a play about Charles Darwin for his bicentenary and the play was premiered at Westminster Abbey. Entitled *Mr Darwin's Tree*, the play ex-plores the life and work of Darwin and has been well received by atheists, agnostics, Christians and people of all beliefs and none around the world. One compelling element in the story, however, is Darwin's beautiful relationship with his wife Emma, who deeply believed in God, while her husband grad-ually moved from nominal Christianity to agnosticism and finally to atheism. Emma would occasionally write loving notes to her husband to challenge him. One letter, which he kept close all his life, pleaded with him to 'consider the chain of difficulties on the other side'. I was very struck by that phrase, because there are at least as many challenges to un-belief as there are to belief in God. Inspired by Emma's 'chain of difficulties', *An Atheist Troubled by His Doubts* is a small contribution to the perennial debate about the existence of God.

I studied the history of art at university and I have always loved paintings of Mary, the sister of Martha and Lazarus, sitting at the feet of Jesus, quietly listening to him. There is no greater occupation than to sit at the feet of the master story-teller and, I think, in the early days of Riding Lights Theatre Company, that's what we were doing when we dramatized so many biblical parables for modern audiences. I continue to reflect on these great parables and *Talent Show* is a 'variation on a theme', born from my experience of struggle, success and failure in the theatre.

Another well-known subject in the history of art is Thomas examining the wounds of Christ, but I have come to understand that the significance of the risen Christ still bear-ing his wounds goes beyond the immense suffering of the Passion. Christ himself carries our wounds and the suffer-ing of the whole of humanity, in profound compassion and total identification. *Love Affair* is a story that expresses this truth.

The Spider Who Believed in Himself is a parable for mil-lennials and for all of us who discover that simply 'believing in ourselves' (a phrase largely unknown before the 1950s) may not be the wisest path through life.

I have spent forty-five years writing and directing plays, working with theatre companies and film producers, writing

3

screenplays and trying to encourage a younger generation in the creative world through workshops and arts courses, so it is in the context of an extremely positive view of all arts and media that I offer the piece *The Angel of Light*. It is when something is essentially good, funny, moving and entertaining that it can also present significant dangers. Interestingly, this piece was written in the late 1980s, before the internet, social media and computer games, and I only had to adapt it slightly for the present time. The argument that there is so much that is good, educational or inspirational in our digital age is not a safe argument when it comes to dealing with the ancient and malign influence described in the Bible as an 'angel of light'.

The Addict is a gentle reminder that going to extremes (as we see in the lives of John the Baptist, Jesus and St Francis, for example) may have something to tell us in our attitude to giving and the stewardship of our material possessions.

Hopefully, anyone who has been kept waiting for long minutes in call centre queues will identify with the emotions (the itching and infuriating grain of sand!) behind the story *The Divine Call Centre*.

Another recent piece is *Cruising Along*. The last hundred years have seen a growing preoccupation with retirement and pension deals in the West and the whole of our society and our outlook on later life have been conditioned by this. In recent years (as I became a 'pensioner' myself), I began to wonder what our early Christian forebears might have thought about this.

I have lived in the far north of Scotland for a long time and the two Christmas pieces were written for carol services at Pulteneytown Parish Church in Wick. *The Lost Angel*, however, could be true of any small town, anywhere in the world. Such towns may seem insignificant but have hidden beauties and glories to offer.

A Little Girl's Letter to God was inspired, many years ago, by the publication of real children's letters to God, which were funny and often very moving. In this piece, I was thinking back to children I knew and loved in the industrial northwest of England. There are so many challenges for children today, but they continue to speak the truth to us: 'unless you become like a little child, you cannot even enter the Kingdom of God.'

The Ultimate Crash has been on my mind for many years, certainly since 2008. Yet, even such an apocalyptic scenario may have something to tell us about what life is really about. As with many of these parables and stories, it has something to say about the arts too – they will always be central to our humanity and our spiritual survival.

The Newcomer was first written many years ago as a sketch for teenagers, in a touring show organized by the Church Pastoral Aid Society. The story of the thief on the cross, in Luke's Gospel, is my favourite story in the whole Bible. Here was a man who had no chance to go off and live a good life. He was doomed. He could do nothing, yet he was saved. It's a story of pure grace. And I couldn't help feeling, when I thought about angels guarding the gates of heaven, that there was considerable comic potential here.

If you read only one story, and take one thought away

from *Yours Truly*, I hope you will make it this last one. Of course, I hope you read them all and that, whatever your beliefs and wherever you are on your journey, this collection offers some laughter and some tears, some light and some joy along the way.

A Celebrity Questions Jesus

A young man, who was a famous celebrity, came to Jesus and said, 'I know you are a very good person and I admire your teachings. Please tell me: how can I find the way to eternal life?'

Jesus looked at him intently. 'No one is good but God.'

The young celebrity smiled, a little uncomfortably. 'Of course, that's a very good point, no one is ever good enough and there is always more we can do to help people – but everyone says that you are the One who really knows the secret of eternal life, so I just thought . . .'

His voice trailed off into the silence. He was not used to a questioning gaze like this. Normally, people smiled and laughed all around him, nodding their heads, agreeing with everything he said and, of course, hordes of people would come waving their cameras, wanting a selfie, desperate for an autograph. Jesus, however, remained very still and there was a deep love in his quiet gaze. The crowd, normally so restless around the celebrity, were hushed into silence.

'You know the Ten Commandments?' Jesus enquired.

'Oh yes,' said the celebrity. '"Do not murder, do not steal, do not tell lies, honour your father and mother . . ." I have kept all these.'

Jesus nodded. He did not challenge the young man at all, but accepted what he said with great respect.

'In fact,' said the earnest celebrity, 'I have tried my very best to live an honourable life. I have given away a lot of money to many charities, I have appeared on *Children in Need* and *Comic Relief* many times, I have worked tirelessly for the Prince's Trust, I have made films for Water Aid and campaigned for refugees throughout the world.'

'Yes,' said Jesus, 'I know, and what you have done is very generous.'

The celebrity smiled for the first time. He was beginning to feel at ease.

Then Jesus moved closer towards him. 'You want to know how to find eternal life?' The question hung in the air for a while.

The celebrity nodded, very thoughtfully. He was deeply sincere in his longing for a good spiritual journey.

'There's only one thing you lack.'

'Oh?' said the young man, now ready to accept some great words of wisdom.

'Give up your celebrity,' said Jesus. 'Go and live among the poor. Do not appear on television ever again. Leave your publicists and your agents and your promoters behind. Give up all your fame and you will have treasure in heaven.'

The celebrity stared at Jesus, utterly astonished. Jesus smiled with great tenderness at him and said, 'When you have done all that, then come and follow me.'

The crestfallen celebrity avoided his gaze. He shook his

head. He walked away slowly, very sorrowfully, because he was extremely famous.

The crowds followed him, and the reporters called out their questions, and the cameras flashed until the celebrity and his entourage had disappeared over the horizon.

But Jesus was still watching, gazing after the young man for a very long time, with tears in his eyes.

An Artist Tries to Create the World

And the artist said, 'Let there be light' and there was light. The artist saw that the light was quite good, but not good enough, so she tried some different colours, but this made it even worse. This was the first day and she was very anxious, because she had a deadline.

And the artist said, 'Let there be a space above the waters' and decided to call it 'sky'. She worked very hard at this and, for a while, she thought it was good. But she came back to it hours later and realized that it was not nearly as good as she had thought. This was the second day and she was beginning to feel panic.

And the artist said, 'Let the dry ground appear' and it was so. Only the dry ground looked far too like the sea and the sea looked like the dry ground, so she completely repainted it. This was the third day and she saw that everything was a disaster.

On the next day, the artist painted the sun and the moon and the stars. And they looked really good, so she decided to paint a whole lot more, which spoilt everything. This was the fourth day and she was contemplating suicide.

And the artist said, 'Let's have a lot of creatures flying

around and swimming in the sea' and some of these were not bad at all. They were actually quite good. This was the fifth day, but she really wanted to paint something much better and she couldn't get the perfect image out of her mind, so she wiped out the whole world and started again.

And on the sixth day, the artist said, 'Let there be light, sky, land and sea, sun and moon and lots of creatures' and she worked in a crazy hurry and the whole thing looked really good, until she realized it was all out of perspective. At this point, she began to drink heavily. Then she remembered that she hadn't created any people yet and she quickly made a man and a woman, but she realized she was no good at human figures. She tried again and again and again, but each time she looked at them, they got worse and worse, so she decided that the whole world she had created was complete rubbish, she was no good as an artist and she would have to become a teacher.

On the seventh day, she woke up with a very bad hangover and she had no rest at all, because she knew that she had to start all over again on Monday.

The Christmas Letter

Eleanor was a good woman. There was no doubting that. Everyone spoke well of her. She was happily married, with three grown-up children, seven grandchildren and a great many friends – and she was a pillar of the local church, always ready to help, always going the extra mile. Some people described her as a saint, but she brushed off such compliments, because she knew she had a long way to go before becoming a saint!

What she didn't know was quite how far she had to go, but she was about to learn.

Eleanor sat down at the beginning of Advent to write her annual Christmas letter. At the top of the letter she placed a large colour photo of her family, all fifteen of them gathered at a family reunion. It was a perfect shot, with everyone smiling and waving and looking radiant in their beautiful clothes.

She began her letter with a few words about Christmas being a time of peace and goodwill in the midst of a troubled world and wishing all her readers a very blessed time. She then said how grateful she was for her family and friends. 'You all mean so much to me!!!' she wrote, adding her trademark three exclamation marks. She then went on to talk about her life with her beloved husband, David, both now in contented 'retirement'. She liked to put 'retirement' in inverted commas, because everyone knew that she and David were hardly retired!!! David, she explained, was running both the Men's Group and the Alpha Group at the church, as well as organizing the Missionary Prayer Breakfast, and he was now also the loyal treasurer of the Local Outreach Committee. There was hardly any time for golf, which he enjoyed so much, but apparently he was improving his handicap nonetheless! She had perhaps taken on a little too much herself, with the Women's Prayer Fellowship, Messy Church, a Lay Reader's Course and becoming a special adviser to the Parent/ Teacher Association at the local primary school. Her days as a primary headteacher were long past, but she loved this involvement very much. Her motto, she wrote, would always be 'Education, Education, Education'.

So 'retirement', she continued, was even less of a reality when it came to her own personal school of seven grandchildren!!! They all had such wonderful characters and needed a lot of love and time, she explained, adding small colour photos of each child as she went along. She then, as she did every year (because it would be awful to miss any of them out), said something encouraging and very complimentary about each of them. So, of course, there were the Suzuki violin lessons, the ballet awards, the swimming certificates, the incredible mountaineering adventures, the clarinet concerts, the scholarship to Cambridge . . . the list was almost embarrassingly long. The truth was, however, that she was very proud of them all and, although looking after the younger ones could be exhausting, or hosting a whole houseful of the entire family last Easter was overwhelming (particularly the quantity of chocolate on offer!!!), she was always grateful for them and was delighted by all the lovely photos they sent to her, which were displayed in every room in the house.

Finally, Eleanor moved on to some of the spectacular holidays that she and David had enjoyed, and how they were enormously grateful to God for these marvellous experiences. She attached a photo of the two of them, looking very young and suntanned, on the deck of a cruise ship in the Caribbean.

It's true that she felt slightly guilty about the five holidays they had enjoyed, although she didn't say this, and she reasoned with herself that they had both worked very hard indeed all their lives for this. But she was careful to put the holidays at the end of the letter, so they could be seen in the context of the tireless work for the church and the demands of family, and so everyone could easily understand why she always put 'retirement' in inverted commas.

Finally, on a more sober and yet joyful note, she ended her Christmas letter, as she always did, with a verse from the Bible and a little homily of hope and joy in these very challenging times. In fact, she was just writing that verse about 'Wonderful Counsellor, Mighty God, Prince of Peace' when she felt a light tap on her shoulder. She turned and was astonished to see a figure standing there, with the most beautiful and radiant face, gazing at her with great sadness.

'Who are you?' she said, suddenly very afraid. The angel said nothing, but just took her by the hand.

Before she could say a word, Eleanor was lifted from the

floor and found herself flying with the angel across the roofs of the city, beneath a brilliant starlit sky. She clung to him for dear life, but he said, 'Do not be afraid, Eleanor. I have been sent to you from the presence of the One who is compassionate, who is merciful, who is all-knowing and who understands all the secrets of the human heart.'

Eleanor found little comfort in these words as her precious home and family vanished to a mere pinprick far below. She was flying in some strange dream-like world. *Have I fallen into a coma? Have I died? Is my life over at last?!!!* Eleanor wondered.

The angel laughed softly, as if knowing every thought. 'Beloved daughter,' he said, 'your life is just beginning.'

That was when they descended and she found herself gently carried through an open window into a small flat. There was a woman, who lived on her own. She had never married or had children. She was sitting, eating a frugal meal from a packet, beside an electric fire with a single bar.

I know this person, thought Eleanor. *She is my old friend from university. It's Ruth! Oh, she seems so sad, so lonely!!!* But Eleanor could not communicate with her old friend, who was completely unaware of her presence or of the burning light around the angel, who stood beside her with tears running down his face.

'Ruth . . . Ruth . . . Are you all right?' Eleanor's words went unheard in that cold and dismal flat, and Ruth continued to stare at a small television, where a comedian was making jokes. But Ruth wasn't laughing. There was an infinite weariness and sadness all around her.

The angel gestured towards Ruth. 'What do you see?' he asked gently.

Eleanor was now in tears. 'I see my old friend Ruth . . . I write to her. I do keep in touch with her.'

The angel looked at Eleanor and his eyes were piercing, bright flames burning her heart. 'How do you write to her?'

'Well . . .' Eleanor hesitated as the deep truth dawned. 'She is on my Christmas list.'

'You send her that letter?' asked the angel.

Eleanor was flustered. 'I . . . er . . . I always write a few hand-written lines at the top, saying, "I hope you are doing well and this comes with much love", that sort of thing.'

The angel was silent for a moment, then said, 'Come on.'

The next thing Eleanor knew, she was flying through the air again, until she landed in a garden. The moon was shining and she stood there outside some French doors, gazing into a beautiful sitting room. But on the sofa, a woman lay weeping and a man sat in a chair with his head in his hands.

'Who are these people?' asked the angel, gently. Eleanor went up to the doors, which swung open mysteriously. Neither of the two troubled figures looked up as she stepped into the room.

'This is Wendy and this is Michael,' Eleanor whispered, hardly daring to breathe their names.

'What has happened to them?' said the angel.

'They, er . . . I believe they lost their baby.'

'Ahh,' the angel nodded, with such terrible sadness and compassion that Eleanor fell to the ground in anguish. Weeping inconsolably, she said:

'They lost their only baby!!!'

'Ohh, ohhh.' Wendy hugged her knees and rocked herself again and again on the sofa. 'Ohhh, my little one.' Michael shook his head and clenched his fists until his knuckles were white. He was paralysed with grief and unable to walk over to Wendy and hold her.

'Let me hold Wendy,' cried Eleanor. 'Let me hold her.'

'Come now,' said the angel and took her firmly by the hand.

'I heard about the cot death and I did write to them,' Eleanor blustered.

'And now you are sending them this letter, at Christmas?'

Tears were streaming down Eleanor's face as they left and flew through the sky. One by one, they visited all the people on her list of two hundred. There were friends who had fallen on very hard times financially and could never afford a holiday, let alone five. There were friends who could never retire, even in inverted commas, because they were self-employed, struggled to survive and had no final salary pensions. There were friends who had children addicted to drugs, and others who had grandchildren who were severely disabled and would never win awards. There were friends who had lost their faith and for whom the trite little homily at the end of Eleanor's Christmas letter inflamed their wounds and increased the bitterness in their souls.

Eleanor could hardly bear one more vision of the harsh reality of human life at Christmas. She longed to love all these people, to plead for their forgiveness, to make a new start.

'Not yet,' said the angel. 'One more visit to make.'

Eleanor found herself flying with the angel over land and

sea, in the darkness and through the mists of time. Slowly, through the unfurling clouds, came a bright and very beautiful star. The angel smiled at her gently, with the saddest and deepest gaze.

'Are we . . . ?' She hardly dared imagine where they were.

'Bethlehem,' said the angel softly, with immense reverence. They flew down, down, into the teeming world of a little town, over two thousand years ago. At last they came to a stable and the angel touched the barn doors, which opened slowly.

Eleanor gazed in wonder, in hope and longing. *Am I about to see the Christ-child myself? To kneel at the foot of the manger? Is this glory to be shared with me?*

As the barn doors opened wide and she stepped into the beautiful and tender scene, she was filled with horror, because sitting in the stable was not Mary, nor Joseph . . . nor the baby, nor the shepherds, nor the wise men.

Eleanor was sitting there herself, beside her husband David. All around were her children and their spouses and her seven grandchildren, including the most recent newborn baby grandson, who lay in the manger. There was a beautiful light around them and they all had halos and were smiling. It was a perfect Christmas scene, with snow lying on the ground outside, the star shining brightly through a skylight high above.

'What do you see?' asked the angel.

'I see . . .' Eleanor hesitated. 'I see . . .' She could not bring herself to say the words, because it was all too terrible.

'What do you see?' asked the angel again, gently persistent.

'I see . . . the Holy Family.'

'Yes,' said the angel, with tears. 'I'm afraid you do.'

There was a long silence as Eleanor gazed at herself and her beloved children and grandchildren, and she knew at last that she had been worshipping her own family, in her most secret shrine, in the deepest place of her heart.

The angel took her by the hand. 'Come.'

His love was so deep and his compassion so full that she followed him, in floods of tears, wondering if this was now the very end of her life, and she was facing the final judgement, or if she was to be spared by some miracle of grace. It was true, she had been worshipping idols of her own making. Far from being a 'saint' she had followed a false religion, the worst kind of all: the religion of the self.

The angel was leading her down a long dark tunnel and, as she stumbled through the darkness, she began to realize that very few of her children and grandchildren believed in God, but every single one of them believed passionately in the family. They had all been converted, from an early age, to an intense and passionate religion – a life-long devotion to the family, to themselves, the radiant glory of their own success, happiness, multiplication and survival. It was a tribal faith that could not endure any rival – above all, the presence of Christ himself at Christmas. That is why the Christmas card, which went with the letter, always had a photo of her own family.

At that moment, Eleanor stumbled into a very dingy room, a hidden stable that was lit by a mysterious inner light. There, in the straw and the poverty, and the muck and the dirt, and surrounded by the poor and the lonely and the destitute and the emotionally shattered and the psychologically wounded and the desperately lonely people, of all ages and all races; there among the refugees of famine, war and faith, and the refugees from comfortable British churches who could no longer endure the self-satisfaction and self-love; there in the midst of the yearning and adoring crowds lay the Christ-child in the manger. Mary sat beside him and her gaze at Eleanor was so full of love, so full of kindness and pure sympathy, that Eleanor fell down and touched the feet of the tiny baby and wept for a long time.

As she did so, it was as if all her sins were sliding away, disappearing, sucked into the blackness and the filth. The radiant inner light that shone from the baby and from Mary and from Joseph and from all the angels who had gathered there, began to shine slowly, very gradually, deep within her heart.

If she could have seen herself kneeling beside the baby, she would have seen a woman bent low with grief but burning with inner light and an imperishable beauty. She would, in fact, have seen a halo.

The last words she heard from Mary were, 'Would you like to hold the baby?' And that was when she found herself back in her own home, with the question ringing in her ears and she found herself whispering, 'Yes.'

In the years to come, Eleanor became famous for her handwritten notes, for telephoning, texting, emailing, messaging and for visiting whenever she could, as many friends as possible, throughout the year. She always communicated personally, speaking with love and insight into each individual situation. And her home, which had been filled with over a hundred photos of her children and grandchildren, now had – alongside a few well-chosen shots of her own family – a hundred pictures of friends she loved and remembered in her prayers. As well as this, she developed a worrying habit of inviting lonely strangers, refugees, troubled teenagers and some awkward misfits from her local church into her home for wonderful hospitality. As a result, her husband David began to play a great deal more golf, which, in its own way, was a special blessing on his life because it gave him the rest and peace he had always needed.

Eleanor considered her new experience, of generous loving and worship, a miracle. Privately, she thought of it as 'holding the baby'.

The truth was, she had discovered the secret of spending her time, throughout the year, being a living Christmas letter, touching countless longing hearts wherever she went.

The Village Secret

Many years ago, a man left his own village in the mountains to visit a town far away. When he got there after weeks of hard and dusty travelling, he quickly discovered that they had the most amazing Secret of Life. Before long, he came to understand the secret for himself and to make it his own. He was filled with excitement and he couldn't wait to rush back and tell the people in his own village – but the guardians of the secret wouldn't let him go.

'Wait here,' they said, 'until you have learnt the right words that must be used when the secret is told to others.' And so he waited for many long weeks, until the words were his. Again, he was keen to be off and tell his friends about the Secret of Life he had found.

'Ah no,' they said, 'for you have many more things to learn . . . People who travel with the secret must dress as we do and put on different clothes to speak about it.' And so he waited, yet again, until he looked exactly as they looked and could have been mistaken for one of them. Once again he urged them to let him go, for the secret was very important.

'Just one more thing,' they said, 'and then you can be on your way. There is a certain kind of behaviour that belongs to the People of the Secret, which you really must learn before you leave us.' So he sat down again to study their behaviour, their customs, their mannerisms, and then, finally, they said to him, 'Now you are ready to go.'

As he hurried over the mountains and down the valleys, his excitement was overwhelming because of what the secret would mean to the people of his village. Finally, after many weeks, his own beloved home came into view, perched high on the mountain he knew so well. He ran towards the village, calling out as he went.

The villagers looked down from the mountain in amazement. Who on earth was this strange-looking man running towards them, shouting so loudly and using such peculiar words? They became very worried and called the village elders, who urged the man to go away. The man shouted all the more, but not a single soul recognized him or understood what he was saying. Finally, as he wouldn't go of his own accord, they took up stones to throw at him, telling him to go away and never come back.

Battered and bleeding, the man set off on the long journey back to the town of the secret, weeping as he went about the rejection he had experienced and the lost opportunity to talk about the secret. When at last he reached the town, the man poured out his story of the bitter experience he had been through, but, to his amazement, the People of the Secret were not surprised.

'You have been persecuted for the secret,' they told him. 'This is part of the price we have to pay. Never mind. Dry your tears and come settle down here with us, where it is safe and where the secret belongs.'

The Plague

The small town of Puffington is a pleasant location, one of the finest in the north-west. The snow-capped peaks of Montana can be seen on the far horizon and the land all around is fertile, with sweeping green pastures in the spring and a carpet of gold at the time of the barley harvest. It was at such a time, not many weeks before Thanksgiving, when something very strange occurred.

There is a large wooden church in the centre of Puffington, beautifully crafted more than a hundred and fifty years ago. The Church of the Redeemer is painted white and gold, with a dazzling cross above an impressive bell tower. White steps lead up to the great wooden doors and nearly all the people of the town file into this majestic place at least once every Sunday.

So it was, in the late 1980s, that they all heard an impressive sermon from their minister, the Revd Milton J. Swackhammer III, who fulminated at great length against the moral evils of American society. They all nodded their heads gravely as he listed the evils of the age: the drug culture, the sexual promiscuity, the blasphemy and violence now rampant in television and film. The whole congregation applauded when he condemned, in the most colourful language, the epidemic of HIV and AIDS as a plague sent by God in judgement on Sodom and Gomorrah.

'This disease,' he proclaimed, 'is nothing less than the outer manifestation of an inner corruption. Every day, sinful men are being exposed, and their vile and secret sins are being revealed in all their hideous deformity! Who can escape from the wrath of God? No one!' He banged the pulpit several times. 'No one, for "The wrath of God is being revealed from heaven against all the godlessness and wickedness of men", Romans chapter 1, verse 18!'

The Revd Milton J. Swackhammer, or 'Rev Milt' as he was known by his loyal congregation, loved the book of Romans, especially chapter 1. In fact, he read it a great deal more than the Gospels and knew it all by heart. 'Men are now, in our time, in our age, before our very eyes' – he didn't mind embellishing Scripture a little now and then – 'receiving in their own bodies the due penalty for their perversion! Romans chapter 1, verse 27.'

Somehow, repeating the chapter and verse out loud gave everything a little extra authority and certainly made him look extremely knowledgeable, because he preached without notes and never once looked down at his large, open Bible. It was as if the words of Scripture flew up, flaming, into his mouth, to be blasted into the vaults of the great Church of the Redeemer in Puffington!

The congregation loved his style, his fervour, his prophetic fury as he lashed contemporary culture time and again. The good people of Puffington would nod their heads, exchange glances and, at frequent moments, applaud and shout out, 'Amen!'

The day of his 'Plague Address', as it came to be known, was warm and sunny, and the people filed out of the church feeling a wonderful sense of well-being. The fruit in the orchards was ripe, the barley harvest was almost ready for gathering, all the businesses, banks, grocery stores, hotels and other businesses were thriving. Puffington was a prosperous place and there was a great deal of cause for rejoicing as the celebration of Thanksgiving drew near. That very Sunday, the church had received its largest collection on record, because the people had been moved by the plight of the nation and the urgent need to spread the message of salvation.

The first peculiar thing that afternoon was a small spot appeared on the church treasurer's forehead. Within hours it had grown and become quite a serious and unsightly lump. His wife called out the doctor and was amazed to see that he too was sprouting a large and very visible lump on his cheek.

'What's happening?' she asked.

'I've no idea,' said the doctor, 'but this is nothing to what is hidden under here.' He rolled up one trouser leg and showed her an appalling sore that extended all the way up his calf.

'Is there a cure?' she said frantically, because now her husband was also rolling up his trouser legs and exposing several bizzare-looking growths.

'I'll need to confer with the hospital of tropical diseases in Missoula tomorrow. This is clearly some kind of . . .' – the doctor hesitated – 'mysterious plague.'

Rev Milt was relaxing in his bath that evening when he was

troubled by the sight of what appeared to be three kneecaps emerging from the foam. Was he dreaming? He swept the foam aside and realized, to his horror, that a very large lump had grown on the side of his left knee. He jumped out of the bath and gazed in the mirror. There was a large spot on his forehead and a hideous lump growing from his ear.

The strange thing was, not everyone in the church was affected. Many of the men grew lumps, and a few of the wealthier women. Puffington's well-respected accountant was one of the worst hit. He had a veritable mountain range of lumps across his bald head.

Experts from the hospital of tropical diseases in Missoula arrived, wearing protective clothing, and examined the unfortunate victims in a special roadside decontamination unit. But this plague was like nothing they had ever seen.

'Can any of you think of anything you have eaten or been in contact with, any plant or animal you have touched?' asked the grim-faced scientist. But the victims shook their heads sadly as they stood in the showers and gazed at their lesions, spots and lumps, which were now multiplying at a terrifying rate.

'We must trust the Lord in this time of terrible crisis!' urged Rev Milt, but even as he said this, a very large lump appeared on his upper lip and he was no longer able to speak.

Puffington was now desperately trying to keep the affliction secret, but it soon became national news that nearly an entire population of highly respectable men, and a small handful of very well-to-do and influential women, were in quarantine. Puffington became known as Plague City.

It was the daughter of the local accountant who, remarkably, broke the spell of this dreadful curse. She was only twelve, but she was very clever and very good with numbers. She had often helped her father in his office and, as he was so severely debilitated (he couldn't sit down because of the multiple lumps on his behind), she was going through his recent accounts for him.

'Daddy!' she exclaimed. 'You've added all the figures up wrongly here!'

Her father stumbled to her side. 'Impossible!' he said, but he was not entirely convincing. 'Add up figures wrongly? What do you take me for?'

'Well,' said the girl, who was very direct and had beautiful clear and honest eyes, 'I would take you for a cheat! You should owe $35,000 to the IRS, but it says here you only owe $7,500.'

'When did I make such a terrible mistake?' blustered her father.

'You did it last Sunday evening,' she said.

With horrible clarity, he realized that the lumps on his head had appeared shortly after he had, not to put too fine a point on it, 'cooked his books'. He immediately rang the church treasurer – the very first victim of the plague.

'Mervyn,' he said, 'can you think of anything you did last Sunday afternoon?'

'What do you mean?' said Mervyn defensively, thinking of the six beers he had drunk before falling asleep in front of the television. 'Having the occasional drink?'

'No, no! Mervyn, think money. Did you do anything regarding . . . church funds, for example?'

'What are you implying?' Mervyn was becoming angry.

'Think about it,' said the accountant. 'It may be your only hope.'

Mervyn sat in his chair and stared into space, for he knew very well that he had, well, borrowed a little money on a short-term loan from the Church Reserve Funds that Sunday afternoon but, of course, he intended to pay it back very quickly, as soon as his cash flow improved.

One by one, the hundreds of victims of the Puffington plague began to discover that the hideous lumps had appeared within minutes of some shady or reckless or unkind or mean or underhand financial act. Ladies who had refused to help a friend in desperate need or disinherited a wayward child to punish them; men who had kept secret accounts to spend on themselves, without their partners' knowledge, or taken out loans to fund a gambling addiction; lawyers, accountants and businessmen who had played fast and loose with each other and with the IRS . . . the list was endless.

The Revd Milton J. Swackhammer III was the very last to face up to the truth. That Sunday, after his thundering condemnation of AIDS victims, he had visited a very wealthy old lady and poured out his heart to her about his desperate need for a brand new car, which was essential to his ministry. He had greatly exaggerated his financial need: he had enough money to buy a new car himself, but not the huge SUV he had set his heart on. She gave him a very large cheque and he prayed with her, fulsomely, thanking God and blessing her for this 'completely unexpected generosity'. He had come home, singing hallelujahs loudly, and run himself a very relaxing bath, which was when the 'third kneecap' had suddenly appeared.

It was the accountant's daughter, of course, who spoke the truth to them all.

'What shall we do?' they said, as if she were a prophet of God (although women were never allowed to speak in the Church of the Redeemer).

'You have to put things right,' she said very simply. 'First with God and then with other people. Who knows? Perhaps he will take pity on us all in Puffington.' They were very touched by the way she included herself in the suffering of the town, even though she was quite innocent. Indeed, the tears in her eyes as she spoke melted all the hardness of their hearts.

The entire quarantined community gathered in the Church of the Redeemer to pray all night for forgiveness. They confessed their sins – not only their secret financial misdeeds but also, above all, their spirit of judgement and harshness towards others.

As they prayed, one by one the lumps disappeared and the lesions vanished and the spots were washed away by a loving invisible hand. Every single man and woman agreed to make restitution to anyone they had cheated or hoodwinked or ignored or condemned unfairly. Rev Milt changed his tune too and was seen humbly welcoming people with AIDS into his home, which became a haven for anyone who was on the margins of faith and had felt wounded and rejected by preachers such as him. When he spoke in the pulpit of the Church of the Redeemer in Puffington, he described himself as a sinner who was desperately in need of grace.

Rev Milt was soon soundly condemned and vilified by a preacher in the nearby town of Vaunting, who described him as an 'ambassador from hell' because of his liberal views.

Needless to say, it wasn't long before Vaunting was visited by a mysterious plague.

The Greatest Discovery in the World

A scientist was working alone in his laboratory for many years. His work often seemed pointless, because his research field was in a very obscure branch of biochemistry. But one amazing day, he began to realize his impossible dream: he had discovered a cure for cancer! He tested the drug many times over and each time, with every variety of cancer, it worked.

He had, at last, discovered the miracle cure that the whole world had been waiting for.

In a moment of crazy enthusiasm, still wearing his white coat, he ran down the local high street, shouting and cheering and, seeing the cancer charity shop, he burst in, laughing.

'Whatever is the matter?' asked the well-dressed lady at the counter.

'Soon you won't need to be here,' he spluttered breathlessly.

'Why ever not?' said the other grey-haired lady, severely.

I should explain that these two redoubtable women had been running the charity shop for nearly twenty years. They had collected hundreds of thousands of pounds in their time. They were extremely proud of their shop.

'Now calm down,' said the elder of the two women, with a kind smile. 'Why do you think we won't be needed any more?'

'Because I have just found the cure for cancer.'

'You have?'

'I really have,' he said, with tears in his eyes. 'It's all over. This is truly a universal cure!'

The old ladies looked at each other in amazement. 'Well, Irene,' said the elder of the two, 'this is a great day and it calls for a celebration!'

'Oh, yes,' said Irene. 'It does indeed. Please come this way. We'll open a bottle of Champagne!'

Smiling, the happy scientist followed them into a back room. There, in the corner, was another door. Irene took the key from a hook high on the wall and opened it. 'Do go in,' she said, ushering the scientist before her.

'This is very kind of you,' he said, but before he could turn round, the door closed behind him. He heard the key turn in the lock.

'What's going on?' he asked, at first quietly and then rather more desperately. He banged on the door. 'Hey, hey, open up!' he shouted, but there was silence.

Gradually, his eyes grew accustomed to the dark. He was surrounded by the bodies of men and women in white coats. One old scientist, clearly on his last gasp, raised a feeble arm. 'Found the cure for cancer, did you? So did I – so did every-one here!'

The eager scientist slowly realized in horror that finding the cure for cancer was not, in fact, good news for everybody.

He banged on the door furiously, but no one came. No one ever came.

Meanwhile, the wonderful ladies kept on running their

charity shop with great kindness and efficiency, and continued to raise thousands of pounds. They were very well respected in the town and they had every intention of keeping it that way.

An Atheist Troubled by His Doubts

There was once an atheist who was troubled by his doubts. It started in small ways. He attended a lecture by a well-known scientist, a famous atheist, and was struck by his intemperate language. In the past, the old familiar scorn for religion had been a source of great consolation to him, but now an awkward question was disturbing him.

If science and reason were so powerfully on their side, why did these celebrated and brilliant men resort to insults, denigration and caricature? Was emotionalism, prejudice, evangelical fervour and bigotry, supposedly the preserve of religious people, also the defining characteristic of many atheists?

Luckily, he was able to put such twinges of doubt behind him, because he was extremely dutiful in his non-beliefs.

Before long, though, other doubts began to assail him. He studied the history of science, which was a serious mistake, as he began to realize that many eminent scientists over the last two hundred years, right up to the present day, believed in God. Of course, a great many did not and he would console himself with this fact but, nonetheless, his doubts began to multiply and breed. He discovered that some of the greatest intellects, including writers, artists, composers, scientists, statesmen, civil rights campaigners and visionaries of the last century, were men and women of deep religious faith. Were they all ignorant fools?

Once again, he turned to his manuals of atheism to reassure himself and strengthen his convictions. He found plenty of invective against corrupt clergy, superstitious adherence to a bankrupt ideology, abusive behaviour and the widespread oppression of the innocent, over thousands of years.

For a while this worked and he fed himself voraciously on a diet of books, pamphlets, documentaries and films, which deeply affirmed his conviction that religion was nothing but fraudulent tales and a tool to manipulate the people. Unfortunately, this train of thought led him to consider Marx's dictum 'religion is the opium of the people' and, before long, he was very unwisely considering the legacy of Marxism and dogmatic state atheism, and the countless millions who had died in the twentieth century as a result of . . . corrupt officials, superstitious adherence to a bankrupt ideology, abusive behaviour and the widespread oppression of the innocent.

His worst moment was when he calculated that far more horror, persecution, death and destruction had been visited on the world in the course of some fifty years than in the whole history of the Christian Church and all religions in several thousand years, and this utter contempt for human life was rooted in a devout atheism that amounted, ironically, to an entirely new state religion.

The atheist did not dare admit these growing doubts to

his friends and relatives, who were all very committed to the creed of non-belief and, for one reason or another, had not thought to question anything very much. One of his best and most comforting ploys, when plagued by private misgivings, was to watch comedians on television who were confident in their atheism and brilliant at poking fun at hypocrisy and, indeed, at almost anything to do with the Church or faith. But it was very upsetting for him to discover that there were also comedians of genuine religious faith rising to the top of the profession and this simply did not fit with his fundamental assumption: funny and clever people are bound to be fellow atheists. In fact, he began to feel betrayed every time he heard of a bright person who had clearly been duped into some kind of primitive religious faith. 'Bright' was a favourite word for many of his intellectual gurus and it had recently become a noun – he liked to consider himself a 'bright'. So encountering very clever people in the arts or sciences who believed in God clearly didn't make sense or, worse, his atheism didn't make sense.

He became quite angry with himself and quite sheepish too as, increasingly, he stopped reading the manuals of faithful atheists and stopped listening so attentively to their invective.

He thought that if he could just forget about all the questions he was having, he could live a peaceful and less intellectually troubled life. He could simply exist. He could do away with arguments and the war of words between atheists and religious people. He could just 'be', which would be the most profound and unashamedly natural way – an animal way – of carrying on with life, enjoying every day as best he could, then accepting death and oblivion.

For, clearly, there was no God and no afterlife.

He repeated these words to himself often, like a mantra, but as he did so, he began to feel that he was whistling in the dark – or, perhaps, in the light?

Perhaps there was a God and there was an afterlife? Was it really irrational and unscientific to believe these things? A significant number of contemporary scientists clearly did not think so. For them, there was no contradiction between faith in God and the pursuit of a scientific career dedicated to open-minded research, new theories and new discoveries.

What harm was there in questioning his old certainties? Surely this was an essential part of a scientific approach to life? But the consequences of such intellectual freedom were disturbing.

The only solace he could find was in not thinking at all because, of course, having a closed mind is a very comforting state of existence. Many dogmatic religious people and many dogmatic atheists have this in common at least. They like to keep a lid on things. But why had his mind become so firmly shut? He would wake up at night sweating, as this question hovered over him like some kind of mischievous spirit sent to torment him. Even the metaphors occurring in his head were becoming a little too spiritual for comfort.

He tried revisiting all the trusty old objections to faith. One of his favourites was the appalling destruction caused by natural disasters, which was a clear indication of a pitiless universe and, obviously, incompatible with any notion of a loving or benevolent deity. However, he came across a very unhelpful book, by a professor of geology, which pointed out that there would be no life on Earth at all without volcanic action, and the existence of every kind of life, from microbes to humanity, depended on forces that are profoundly creative, as well as blindly destructive. The professor went on to point out that rich people survived earthquakes and eruptions far better than the poor, and there were glaring moral issues of global justice, construction methods and early warning systems that had to be addressed, as natural disasters are an inextricable part of life on Earth.

All this did not deal with the terrible anguish of human suffering, but it framed the question in a different way. Given the realities of life on Earth, including dramatic changes in weather patterns, rising sea levels and an increasing number of forest fires, almost certainly due to the reckless exploitation of natural resources, the human race has an urgent moral imperative to think, act and plan differently. Otherwise, the greatest natural disaster of all, the extinction of life on this planet, will be caused by the most extreme and destructive force in the whole of nature, which is humanity itself.

The atheist sincerely wished that he hadn't read this paradoxical book and hurled it across the room, where it continued to stare at him, accusingly, from a flower pot.

The best and easiest solution, he decided, was simply to slump into an armchair and watch the news and see all the violent troubles in the world – clearer evidence of all the random brutality of existence. However, even this perennial 'problem of evil' argument became a little more complex when he began to ask, 'Why should we care about pain and death, as it is all part of an evolutionary struggle? Why should we feel, deep down, that torture and murder are terrible injustices? And why do people intervene and try to change things? Where do acts of selfless bravery and altruism come from?'

The relentless questions were mounting day by day, and he was sure there were good scientific answers for them. In fact, many great thinkers were working hard on the altruism problem and had come up with some good biological parallels and, generally speaking, reasonable 'explanations'. But no one had yet observed chimpanzees collecting money for chimpanzee orphans they didn't know thousands of miles away. Research was in its early days. All this was unsettling, because the last thing in the world he wanted to consider was any kind of goodness or innate moral law or, worse, some kind of essential spiritual identity that might point to . . . the existence of a creator. Men and women made in the image of God!

Such a belief would be the worst possible outcome, certainly for his atheism.

The final and most troubling doubt, which came at him like a hammer blow, occurred when he was watching a television documentary about the origins of the universe. Normally, this was completely safe territory. The vastness and meaninglessness of the universe, ironically, made good sense to him. But then along came this absurd nuclear physicist who pointed out the fact that if the rate of expansion of the universe, one second after it came into existence, had been smaller by even one part in a hundred thousand million million, it would have collapsed and 'we would not be here to make this programme'. The humble and smiling scientist had gone on to say, as if he was pleased with all this outrageous improbability, 'This is about the same accuracy needed to hit a coin at the other side of the universe fifteen million light years away.'

This was unhelpful. It certainly ruined the atheist's evening. It wasn't the graphic and infuriating simplicity of this image; it was the train of thought it led to . . . for hours and hours . . . for days and days.

He now had far too many doubts to handle and it was time to take action. It was time to avoid thinking for ever. It was time to firmly close his mind again but, like some ancient misshapen door, his mind would not shut completely. It kept creaking open and there was a freezing cold draught coming through.

He had always loved the 'multiverse' theory – that there were an infinite number of universes and so all things were possible, in any combination, in any number of dimensions. But, of course, and rather awkwardly, this could not be proved by strict scientific examination because these endless universes were not open to study and could only be inferred. They were in fact, in some significant way, an article of faith.

And here's how the final questions brutally assaulted him: did it take more faith to believe in a creator who was outside time and space and not subject to the laws of the known universe than it did to believe in an infinite number of other universes that had arisen entirely from nothing? Or arisen from the minds of atheists who simply could not stomach the idea of a creator and had to find a viable alternative at the very least?

But then, supposing the attractive 'multiverse' theory were true after all, did it really abolish the idea of a creator or did it imply, even more insistently, that there must be one? For if the vast nothingness that lay behind all existence was effectively a womb of cosmic creativity, how did one account for this? It was surely a remarkable and unparalleled leap of the imagination – a scientific faith of infinite degree – that would be needed to believe all matter and all organic life and every conceivable universe simply jumped out of 'nothing'.

Of course, the atheist would often repeat the familiar twenty-first-century argument to himself, rehearsing it in the mirror and declaring it to any wavering agnostic friends in the pub: 'The universe appearing from nothing is not a problem! In the microcosmic sphere of quantum mechanics, particles such as protons can appear and disappear at random. They leap out of nothing, they can vanish suddenly and reappear somewhere else from nothing, so why not the universe itself? Since the universe was originally no bigger than a proton, why couldn't the whole damn thing be just a blip appearing out of nothing?'

In this way, life, the universe, all universes, all matter, every insect and animal, every human being, all works of art, all inventions and scientific discoveries, all loving and caring, every single act, good, bad or indifferent, and all human consciousness that enables humankind to explore the universe and, indeed, watch protons appearing from nothing come from . . . nothing.

He would breathe a sigh of relief whenever this fundamental fact stared at him once again, like a familiar friend. Nothing! It was reassuring.

But unfortunately, his febrile mind, disturbed by a maddening TV documentary, refused to calm down or shut down, and questions still came tumbling out of the void.

Surely this precious concept of 'nothing' would have to be a fixed and immutable reality for eternity? There was no room for a later generation of scientists to discover that what was previously thought to be nothing was, in fact . . . something.

For, as one scientist had put it, 'the latest word in science must never be the last word'. But in this case it had to be! Nothing would have to remain an all-powerful reality. Beyond time and space itself. Because, otherwise, where did the laws of nature – mathematics, physics and chemistry – come from, which everything after the Big Bang had so faithfully observed? Obviously, from nothing.

Nothing. Omnipotent. Eternal. In fact, a bit like God, without the church bit.

The more the atheist contemplated the remarkable creative power of nothing, the more he began to realize that here it was again. Faith. Impressive, monumental, infinite – supreme faith, rather than reason, was ultimately required for him to believe that everything came from absolutely nothing. He did not have this gift, however, although he wished, with all his heart, that he did, because he greatly valued his atheism and the freedom and independence it gave him, not to mention the intellectual respect staunch atheism could offer in today's Western world. He was even beginning to say to fellow atheists, deeply, sincerely, 'I wish I had your faith.'

But he couldn't find it. He couldn't reach it. He couldn't inflate the tiny mustard seed, the human faculty of faith he still possessed somewhere deep inside, to such a vast, improbable size.

'Mustard seed' . . . he'd heard that somewhere before.

The mustard seed of faith.

This tiny and mysterious force now sparked into life from the apparent nothingness of his soul. A voice seemed to be whispering to him, faintly audible in the darkness of his despair, 'My child, why wrestle with doubt any longer? A mere quark of faith in me will do, and this will soon move the mountain of irrational scientific faith that is now crushing your soul. And, by the way, you do have a soul. I took a great deal of loving care making it.'

At this, the atheist started to hum loudly to himself in the hope of silencing his disordered imagination. He clearly needed psychiatric help. There was probably a drug somewhere that was available to silence 'still small voices' or other psychotic experiences. Surely there was a neuroscientist who could help here? However, even his considerable faith in medical science was beginning to crumble. Something unexpected and very awkward was happening. He was in unfamiliar territory, which is always a dangerous place to be.

He went out for a very long run, across meadows and fields, jogging for hours until the night sky appeared in all its glory, but he avoided looking at it, because it was gradually filling with meaning and extraordinary hope.

His head was hurting, all because of a ridiculous and ephemeral little documentary. He sincerely hoped that the profound upset he was now feeling in his head, his stomach, his heart and possibly even his soul, would pass.

But it didn't.

The supremacy of nothing, the self-explaining cosmos, an infinite number of universes erupting from nowhere, along with a great many other elements in the expanding creed of atheism, clearly required a macrocosmic leap of faith.

He could no longer make such an interstellar jump. This was terrible news for his formerly devout beliefs.

In fact, the atheist was forced to rely almost entirely on reason and science, which is how he lost his faith and became a Christian.

Talent Show

A businessman had four employees.

As he was going away for a long time, he gave each of them some money to invest.

To the first he gave £100,000. To the second he gave £50,000, to the third he gave £25,000 and to the fourth he gave £10,000.

When he came back after a year, he called them into his office one by one.

The first employee explained, 'I invested your £100,000 in a variety of enterprises and they have all proved very successful. I have made you a million pounds.'

The businessman was overjoyed. 'You have done brilliantly and now I will promote you to high office and give you a large bonus and a great deal of responsibility. We'll celebrate your success with a wonderful party.'

The second employee explained, 'I invested your £50,000 in several enterprises and I played the stock market successfully. I have made you £250,000.'

'Congratulations,' said the businessman. 'I knew I could trust you. You will receive promotion and a bonus and be invited to a wonderful party to celebrate.'

The third employee came to him a little sadly and said, 'I invested your £25,000 in putting on a play. The play was outstanding and got good reviews. Many people were deeply moved. But I am afraid that times are very difficult in the arts world and the play did not transfer anywhere, so I lost all your money.'

'Nonsense,' said the businessman. 'You didn't lose a thing. You touched people, you blessed them. That's riches enough. You tried your hardest, you acted with courage and I love fearless risk-taking more than anything. I consider my £25,000 well spent. Tell me about your future projects and I will give you greater backing and more responsibility, and you must come to my party to celebrate.'

Finally, the fourth employee came in. He was smiling. 'Here is your £10,000 back, safe and sound.'

The businessman was astonished. 'What happened to it?'

'Like I said,' explained the employee, 'nothing at all. Here it is, safe and sound.'

'You didn't even put it into a savings account and at least earn a little interest?'

'Oh no, sir, that's hardly worth doing in the current state of the economy. I just put the cash in a safe and kept it there.'

By now the businessman was becoming furious. 'You didn't even risk my money on some worthy venture?'

'I didn't want to do that,' said the employee, shocked. 'Look at what happened to your employee who lost every penny! He just squandered everything on a doomed artistic production. At least I am returning your investment in perfect condition.'

Now the businessman was extremely angry. 'You're fired,' he said, 'and I will never give you a reference. You will never work in this city again. You're a loser.'

'But,' the employee protested, 'I didn't lose anything!'

'You lost your nerve,' said the businessman, 'and now you've lost your livelihood and your reputation.' With that he called security and the man was hurled out on to the street, and all his possessions with him.

'Bring me men and women who are enterprising, who work hard, who try anything and take risks,' said the businessman. 'In my company, the worst failure is to play safe and do nothing.'

Love Affair

A young woman discovered that her husband was having an affair. She asked him how he could have done this to her and he said, 'This would never have happened if you had loved me enough. This is your fault as well as mine.'

She ran out of the house in terrible distress until, at last, she came to her parents' house. She poured her story out to her mother, who put her arm round her and said, 'You must try to win him back. You must buy better clothes, start wearing more make-up and take much better care of yourself. A man doesn't want a woman who looks dull and dreary. That is why he has started to look elsewhere.'

In anger and despair, the young woman walked away from her parents' house, weeping even more bitterly. A friend saw her staggering along the street and took her by the hand. 'What on earth is the matter?' she said. 'What dreadful thing has happened to you?'

The woman could not speak for a long while, so the friend made her sit down on a park bench. 'Calm yourself,' she said. 'Tell me everything.'

The woman poured out her story once again and explained how her husband had met a younger woman at work and had been secretly having an affair for two years.

'He's a wicked and selfish man,' said her friend. 'You must get your own back on him. Have an affair yourself and he will soon see what he has lost.'

'I love him,' said the young woman. 'There is no one else I want.'

'He will never come back to you,' said her friend, 'unless you treat him in exactly the same way that he treated you. Then he will come running.'

The woman left her friend in great confusion and, everywhere she looked, there were handsome men in the street, glamorous posters and alluring images on magazine covers. The whole world seemed to be shouting, 'You're still young. There are plenty of other men, it's time you took your revenge.' She was so overwhelmed by the clamour of her thoughts that she wandered into an empty church and sat down on a pew deep in shadow.

She cried quietly for a long time until a kindly priest came up to her. 'I'm sorry to disturb you,' he said, 'but you seem to be in trouble. Is there anything I can do to help?'

Reluctantly, she told the priest what had happened and why she was now sitting alone in such great sorrow. He shook his head. 'This is one of the most painful things that can happen to anyone and there are no easy answers. But you must learn to forgive him, because we have all committed great sins, even if they are just in our hearts, and no one is innocent.' He went on to tell her the story of the woman taken in adultery in John's Gospel and how all her accusers had left one by one, convicted of their own sin. 'You must not condemn your husband,' he said. 'You must forgive him.'

The woman nodded in silence, but as she walked out of the church into the sunlight of the busy street, she did not feel any peace. In fact, the words of the kindly priest seemed to weigh her down like a huge stone laid on her heart. She felt angry and sad all at once. If forgiveness were the way forward, she felt beyond all hope, because her mind was tormented with images of her husband and his lover, at every corner, in every pub, in every passing car. Her emotions boiled like the darkest sea in a storm.

It was then that she saw a figure she knew well walking out of a hairdresser's salon, looking young, beautiful and very confident. Her husband's lover looked her in the eye and said coldly, 'I'm sorry about what has happened, but it's not my fault.'

The young woman wanted to shout and scream and punch her husband's lover, who was already walking away, but her mouth was dry and she felt almost paralysed with the shock of what was now becoming a horrible reality. She blurted out after her, 'Whose fault is it?'

'You must ask yourself that,' said the lover, without turning back.

The young woman now wandered alone for hours and the rain started to beat down in the darkness. She stumbled onwards, not caring where she was going, not caring if she lived or died. The wind and the rain were howling around her as she walked a long way out of the town and down a forgotten country road. She had no idea where she was going, because all she could hear were voices inside her head telling her that it was all her fault and all she could see in her mind were images that tortured her very soul. She was neither seeing nor hearing anything in the world around her, so lost was she in her thoughts, until she came to a lonely hill that was scarcely visible in the gathering night.

There was a tree in the darkness, which she clung to, although she did not know why. It seemed so strong and very ancient and, as she collapsed at the foot of the old tree, she felt something dripping on her head. It was not water, although the rain was still beating down. It was blood. She looked up, astonished and very frightened, to see a figure hanging high up the tree. Suddenly, a flash of lightning revealed a face gazing at her in such tremendous sorrow and love, she broke down, weeping and weeping, until she could cry no longer. She lay there, hardly daring to gaze any more, shaking and unable to speak.

The man on the tree spoke to her with such softness that she could hardly hear him. She listened to the voice, which came between deep and agonizing breaths. 'Daughter,' he said, 'my beloved.' She clung to his feet, which were covered in blood and cruelly nailed. 'You see these wounds? Do you know how they came to be?' She shook her head. 'They are yours,' he said, as he attempted to breathe, clearly in great pain. He moved his right hand as much as he could, curling his fingers. 'Your husband gave me this,' he said, 'when he blamed you for his own sins.' He moved his left hand. 'Your mother gave me this when she told you that you were not beautiful enough.' He looked down at the blood streaming from the great gashes in his feet. 'This nail was driven in by your friend, who tempted you to harm yourself with bitterness and revenge. This nail was driven in by the priest who laid the burden of forgiveness on your broken spirit before you were ready to bear it.' Finally, blood and water came flowing from his side. 'This is the last wound,' said the man, 'delivered by the woman who spoke to you from the hardness of her heart and whose self-righteousness is even greater than all the others. She will destroy anyone in the name of her own happiness and consider herself justified.'

At that moment, the man arched his back on the tree and called out in a loud voice, 'Father, forgive them, for they don't know what they are doing.'

Suddenly, there was a great earthquake, the ground shook and huge clouds roared across the sky, which was filled with lightning and then total darkness.

The young woman lay at the foot of the tree, holding it closely, weeping softly and then suddenly felt so light in her spirit that she fell asleep, like a newborn baby. She slept for a very long time – it seemed like a whole day and half – and then she awoke with the first rays of a new dawn. The tree had gone and she found herself beside an ancient tomb with a huge stone lying flat on the ground nearby, as if the great weight of death had been pushed aside, almost casually, like a leaf or a pebble tossed to one side by a storm.

A figure was seated beside her. She knew who it was from the terrible scars in his feet. His arms were round her and he held her for a long time in the stillness of the garden as the birds sang and the rays of the sun warmed her face. He cradled her head in his lap, he ran his fingers through her hair and he said to her softly, 'You are very beautiful.'

She gazed up at him, the tears now dry on her cheeks, and he nodded. 'Go,' he said. 'Go, my daughter. Your pain will always be mine, and mine will always be yours. Go into all the world and, from now on, listen only to the sound of *my* voice singing in your heart.'

The Spider Who Believed in Himself

There was once a very young and headstrong spider. He never listened to his parents and teachers or anyone in authority. He was determined to find his own path through life, in his own way and in his own time. He was determined to believe in himself, above all things, and find authenticity in as many different adventures as possible. He had watched all the spider films and listened to all the spider songs and even been to the Arachnid Olympics, where his spider heroes had all said the same thing: 'You just need to believe in yourself and you can achieve anything you want.' For a long time, this philosophy suited him well and he would weave his webs in the most daring places and catch more flies than any other spider in his class. He dreamed of winning gold medals for Perfect Stillness and Deception and, one day, the World Championships for 'Bluebottle Catching'.

His parents loved him very dearly, but nothing they said could persuade him to take a little more care with his young and precious life. There was one particular and fearsome hazard that had cost the life of his grandfather and several cousins. His mother and father had only the vaguest idea of the peril that lay beyond, but they knew that this dreadful place lay somewhere through the Great Dark Pipe.

'Don't ever go there, son,' his father had warned repeatedly. 'You will disappear for ever, like my father!'

'Yes,' his mother pleaded gently, 'don't listen to all the dares and bravado of your friends! No young spider has ever made it back from the Great Dark Pipe and others have returned shrivelled and crushed and drowned. It's horrible! I have seen the ruin of many young and rebellious spiders.'

The young spider smiled to himself, clearly ignoring these old-fashioned warnings from his aged parents. Naturally, the Great Dark Pipe held a deep and fatal fascination for the teenage spider (he was all of fifteen weeks old). He had climbed up high buildings, built precarious webs from crumbling rafters and swung clean and low from rusting tractors. He had even woven his gossamer magic between door handles and doorposts, although these escapades had nearly cost him his life. Somehow the thrill of danger, of every new and unpredictable adventure, intoxicated his young mind. He became convinced, day by day, that the Great Dark Pipe would be his ultimate conquest.

One night, he scuttled away from all his friends and family and, through a narrow gap, entered the very lowest curve of the mysterious and shadowy Great Dark Pipe. He began to climb and it was remarkably calm and still. There were no hazards, only a few drops of water, and, in fact, the damp made it so much easier to ascend smoothly. At one point, he heard a great sound of water flowing somewhere far away, a terrible din, but nothing came down the pipe and he slowly continued right to the very top.

The intrepid young spider squeezed out of some fine mesh and found himself on a vast and silent sloping world, lit only by a far-off moon. He explored as far as he could, right and left, forwards and backwards, but to his slight consternation he found he couldn't climb up to the top at all. He then realized, in this hard white wilderness, that he was lost. It was almost unknown for him to feel panic, but the fear that started to overwhelm him now was unfamiliar and deeply disturbing. He began to long for old rafters and skirting boards and door posts and forgotten corners in garden sheds, as he found himself sliding down, once again, into the cold whiteness.

Why couldn't he climb up to the edge, which he could sense sometimes so near and yet always so far? Why couldn't he retrace his steps? He could no longer find the forbidden entrance to this bleak and terrible place.

Just then, a light snapped on and the whole world was filled with a blazing and dreadful brightness. Instinct told him to stay quite still, so he did – he was very good at that. He stayed perfectly still and he was prepared to remain like that until it became dark again. He desperately wanted to try one more run up the smooth sides, but he knew extreme danger when he saw it.

Something vast was looming above the cold and cruel world he had entered.

A voice screamed and he froze with utter terror. 'Aaaargh!' came the cry. 'Aaaargh!'

Another shape loomed in the glare of this harsh universe. 'Spider, is it?'

'Kill it! Kill it!' the voice continued to scream. 'Wash it down! Wash it down!'

There was a dreadful silence as the little spider sat there, utterly still but completely exposed, and for the first time in his short life he knew there was nothing at all he could do. He did not dare admit it, but he was helpless and the slow, tormenting realization came to him that believing in himself was not enough. It could not save him.

If only the darkness would come. If only he could find his way back to the Great Dark Pipe, which now seemed so comforting and so inviting.

But there was no chance of that. Everything now lay in the hands of some other vast beings – everything had become their choice, their belief, their will.

'Kill it! Kill it!' the voice pleaded again. 'Get rid of it!'

'No,' said the gentler, deeper voice. 'No, I will not kill him. He deserves to live too, you know!'

With that, a huge hand came down and, as it did so, as the shadow fell on the little spider, he was forced to run for his life, high up the white walls, down again, high up, down again, but nowhere, nowhere could he escape, and the deep and gentle voice said, 'Come on, little one' as the vast being finally caught him in his cupped hands. The spider felt the rush of air and the sheer terror of unexpected flight, out of his control, far beyond all he had ever known.

'I'll pop him out of the window,' murmured the deep and caring voice and, with that and another rush of cool air, the hand lowered the little spider on to the fresh grass and the flowers covered with dew.

The window closed. The voices receded. And the spider found himself in the most beautiful garden, with plenty of food and a thousand holes to hide in, under stones and in sheds, and a myriad of branches where he could weave his daring webs once again.

His parents and friends and brothers and sisters watched with horror as a flood of water came down the Great Dark Pipe and, for all they knew, he was lost for ever.

Meanwhile, as the young spider began his new life in the sunshine, there was a strange peace flooding his body and giving new energy to all of his eight legs. He no longer believed just in himself. He no longer believed he could fulfil all his dreams and do whatever he chose without help. He truly believed that there was someone else out there, far bigger and far kinder than he had ever imagined.

The Angel of Light

One day, a radiant figure came flying through the cosmos. He was beautiful and charming and spoke with the most soothing and persuasive voice you have ever heard. Some called him 'the Prince of the Power of the Air' because he ruled the airwaves and his media kingdom was without equal in power and influence. He was the greatest writer, actor, singer and film-maker all rolled into one, for he knew the secret of inspiration and gave his wisdom freely to all who would listen.

His other name was the 'Angel of Light' and he had many apartments and offices around the world, from Hollywood to London, from Mumbai to Beijing. His business interests flourished, from Silicon Valley to Nairobi and from the highest places in the land to the humblest child's bedroom on a deprived estate. Wherever there was a screen, a phone, a games console, an app, a connection, the Angel of Light could be found smiling and making himself at home. It is fair to say that he was the most skilful dramatist in the known universe and his greatest ambition was to create a parallel universe of the imagination that would endure for ever.

One day, he decided to give a rare and honest account of his philosophy and artistry in film, and this is how he addressed the human race:

I will create an imaginary world that you can comfortably inhabit. I will invite you into my world with laughter, beauty, pathos and haunting music. You will be laughing so loud, you will be crying so much, you will be so involved with the characters I create and so hypnotized by the images I pass before your eyes, you will not notice that it is a world without God.

It is a world where there is morality but not absolute morality: what is right or wrong will depend on the needs of my heroes or my heroines. For they will be alone again in the Eden of my imagination and they will eat freely of the Tree of Knowledge of Good and Evil, so much that they will become like gods.

The protagonists in my drama will have no authority higher than their own happiness. So, whatever goes wrong for them will be a tragedy; whatever goes right for them will be a comedy, a celebration of love.

I will enrich their characters at every turn at the expense of others. If they admit adultery, I will not allow you to enter deeply into the lives of their victims. I will drain these other characters of life, of humour. I will make them ciphers, ridiculous stereotypes: I will show you how shallow fools clearly deserve to be cheated on and deceived. Or I may show something deeper – something more painful in the consequences of human desire – but, if I do, I will move you by the pain and anguish in the hearts of my heroes. You will see how they suffer for forbidden love and, ultimately, you will always pity them.

My Adam and Eve will never know sin or responsibility for their actions, because they will be gods.

I will lure you into my imaginary world with bright lights, with the splendour of nature, with the exquisite beauty and erotic power of the human body. Oh yes, I will borrow everything I need from God's world.

But I will banish his presence. With the flaming sword of my imagination, I – the Angel of Light – will stand at the gates of my Eden and guard them jealously from the entry of the truth.

Yet, I will always welcome you, tempting you into my garden with little scraps of truth. I will offer you edited highlights of the spiritual world, God's world, speeches about justice, war, love, forgiveness, moments of moral insight, jewels of inspiration – in such a way that you will never notice how many people were killed in the name of justice, how many families were ruined in the name of love.

You will be thrilled by the speed, the drama, the electrifying pace of my world, dazzled so you will not care or stop to reflect for a single instant.

You will be mine.

You will laugh, perfectly on cue, when I create yet another simpering vicar or ludicrous bishop or hypocritical evangelist. When I cuckold yet another bald-headed old fool or uptight, uncaring wife.

You will applaud when more faceless, characterless extras are amusingly blown to smithereens.

You will not reflect.

You will glory in violence, because it has no consequence and no meaning.

You will burn with self-righteous indignation at tales of corrupt priests and cruel nuns and sinister cardinals. You will know, without a shadow of doubt, that you yourselves are never corrupt, never cruel and never lie to save your own skins. For you will always fight for the truth – my truth.

You will not reflect.

You will walk tall above the predators and the abusers, and you will celebrate the documentaries and the exposés of hypocritical celebrities and their shameful self-love, and you will never once look into the mirror of your own soul.

You will not reflect.

You will be mine. And better, far better, your children will be mine. For they will have drunk my delicious cocktail of truths and half-truths, of morality and immorality, of heroes who are absolved of their sins because they are so beautiful and they have loved so tenderly and murdered only in the name of justice.

Your children will hold hands with my Adam and Eve, in the cool of my garden, and God will not come to them.

There will be no judgement, no mercy; no moral law, no forgiveness. No love.

There will only be me.

Because while God's people were sleeping, I crept into the world and stole all the children. I carried them through silver screens, through laptops and tablets and smartphones and computer games, through apps and social media, through box sets and soaps and sitcoms, through magazines and adverts and films.

I took them all into my garden.

I led them there laughing.

I entertained, I thrilled them.

I blinded them with my beauty.

The Addict

A woman was walking through her local park when she saw a man lying under a newspaper on a park bench. He was in a desperate state but, surprisingly, he offered her his newspaper and asked if she would like to read it.

'No, thank you,' she said. 'You need everything you've got.'

'No, really,' he insisted. 'Please have it! I've got the colour supplement here as well. Take it all!'

She was flustered when she realized that he had no clothes on at all under the newspaper. 'Oh no, honestly,' she smiled as politely as she could. 'Your need is greater than mine.'

'How do you know?' he said. 'There might be an advert in this paper for the perfect job, an article that could change your life.'

'Really,' she said, nervously pushing the newspaper back towards him. 'I'm fine as I am.' He covered himself with the newspaper again and she relaxed enough to sit down beside him. 'But what about you? Do you have anywhere to sleep tonight?' She was determined to help him if she could.

'No, just this park bench,' he said. 'Luckily, it's bolted to the ground and it belongs to the council, otherwise I wouldn't even have this.'

He was clearly an unusual character, but she could see his

situation was desperate. He had literally nothing in the world. 'Tell me,' said the woman, overflowing with sympathy, 'how did your life come to this?'

The man was silent for a moment, but her kind and patient presence was reassuring. Finally, the sad tale of his terrible addiction came pouring out.

'It started small,' he said. 'I knew it was wrong. I used to give small gifts to people, the odd sweet here and there. A bunch of flowers, a bar of chocolate. But then it escalated. I gave five pounds to a homeless man and I couldn't stop. Soon I was a Registered Giver. I set up standing orders to many charities. I started reading the Gospels. Somebody said they liked my coat, so I gave it to them – and my suit jacket as well.

'I had cognitive behavioural therapy sessions and I was advised to put a ten pound note in the collection bowl and treat that as my entire giving for the week, but it didn't work. I kept emptying my pockets and then making payments for large amounts. I knew I had let the therapist down and I stopped going because I felt guilty.

'I was so desperate I sought help at many churches and, for a while, I was greatly comforted by a large city church where people were obviously very rich, but gave almost nothing away. There was hope at last, but then I had a terrible relapse.

'I met someone, a preacher from an American church, who told me that "the Lord is no man's debtor" and, if I gave money away generously and sacrificially, the Lord would pay back double. That is exactly what happened. The more I gave away, the more money kept rolling in and I found that I had to give away more and more. It was a nightmare. I got into a terrible downward spiral.

'Eventually, I found two credit counsellors who were full of good sense. They knew what was good for me: complete and utter selfishness. They showed me how to keep all my money. They persuaded me to become a total miser, but it was no use. One day, I just ran off and gave away the books and DVDs they had shared with me. I went on a complete binge. I bought a thousand copies of the *Big Issue* in one afternoon. I felt compelled to give away something every hour of the day and if I didn't, I would suffer from agonizing withdrawal symptoms.

'Finally, I knew I had to go into rehab and I went to a remarkable place called the Friary, which is run by ex-Franciscans who have bravely faced their extreme addiction. Now, many of these former monks drive expensive cars and live in luxury. I felt there was a bright light at the end of the tunnel. I hung on every word of wisdom, I attended all the sessions that took place over seven-course meals. For a while I felt an incredible sense of hope, but then it happened. A craving, a longing.

'I sneaked out one afternoon to the local town and I just gave away a few pounds here and there: one pound fifty to a busker, two pounds to an Albanian woman begging, five pounds to the Salvation Army. I really couldn't stop myself. I ran into the local library, to see if I could calm down and find a book that would teach me how to be completely mean and selfish. I was just thumbing through the autobiography of a famous businessman, when I saw a book on the life of St Francis. That is what destroyed everything.

'I took the book back to the Friary which, of course, had totally banned this dangerous work. I kept it under my pillow and I read it many times over. I went home, put my house on the market, sold it for a great deal of money, gave everything away, sold all my clothes and possessions on the internet and then walked naked into this park. Somebody gave me this newspaper, but I feel awkward having it.'

The kindly woman stood up, profoundly shocked at everything she had heard. She knew this man was completely beyond help. His condition was extremely serious and certainly very contagious. If she stayed there a moment longer, she would be in danger of giving away her handbag on the way home and goodness knows what else. She might be arrested for indecent exposure. She began to walk away hastily.

The addict called after her, 'I don't suppose you've got the price of a cup of tea, madam?'

'No!' she said sternly. 'Because you'll just give it away to someone else.'

'You're right,' he smiled. 'I can't help myself.'

The Divine Call Centre

There was a very successful businessman who made a fortune in the telecommunications industry. Like many brilliant entrepreneurs, he started out humbly, offering a telephone advisory service and handling all the calls himself. Gradually, he increased staff and multiplied offices and soon his company was helping thousands of people daily. As mobile phones, the internet and all varieties of social media began to proliferate, he then had to outsource much of his work to call centres around the world. Finally – and he was very proud of this – he was one of the very first global companies to develop algorithms that could deal with millions of customers simultaneously using the most advanced computer technology.

It was amazing. He hardly needed people any more – computers did everything, including offering highly technical advice. He floated the company on the stock market and made $1.5 billion in a single day.

Soon after this happened, however, now retired and living in a huge villa in the south of France, things began to go wrong. His wife left him and sued him for a huge sum as a divorce settlement, his youngest daughter became very ill and the tax authorities launched an investigation into his finances, all at the same time.

It was a sweltering hot day and he wandered down the street in utter loneliness and desperation. For the first time in his life, he found himself going into an old church, where he sat down beneath a stained-glass window and gazed curiously at the depiction of angels ascending and descending above a man who was sleeping on a stone pillow. He had no idea what this story was about, but he felt some sympathy for the strange figure, lying there in a barren desert, and he wondered how so many angels came to be there, all visiting him in person, one by one. It was a beautiful and touching sight and it brought tears to his eyes – tears of sympathy and desperation.

He found himself trying to pray. He called out to the Almighty, 'Oh God, if you exist, please hear my prayer. I'm in a whole lot of trouble and I need you now.'

He was astonished to hear a voice high above, in the stillness of that beautiful church. The voice rang out, loud and clear, 'Hello. Your call is in a queue and your query will be answered within two minutes.'

He was stunned. He looked around everywhere, but could see no one. He began to think his mind was going, in the midst of all his desperate troubles, but then the voice came again, in a soft and pleasing American accent, saying, 'Your call is important to God. Please don't hang up.'

He looked up wildly and the angels were still quietly ascending and descending to the lonely figure. If only he could see an angel for himself! If only a divine figure would come down now, solve his financial problems, heal his poor suffering daughter! Just then, he glanced in front of him and, instead of a Bible or a hymnal on the pew, he noticed there was a keypad.

The voice spoke again: 'Press 1 if you have problems with your family, press 2 if you have financial problems, press 3 if you are suffering from an illness, press 4 if you are depressed.'

He didn't know why, but he pressed 4. He was certainly feeling very desperate inside. The voice came again: 'Press 1 if you feel a vague sense of unease, press 2 if you feel desperate, press 3 if you feel utter despair, press 4 if you feel suicidal.'

He stormed out of the pew, shouting and swearing. 'What kind of answer is this?'

Undeterred, the voice repeated blandly: 'Your call is important to God. Please don't hang up.' Suddenly there was a crackle on the line, then a buzzing sound and then there was another voice, this time a female one with a British accent, who said pleasantly, 'Your call is in a queue and it will be answered in less than ten minutes.'

Enraged, he hurled the keypad across the marble floor, smashing it to pieces. 'What kind of God is this?' He began to storm out of the church. 'Is this how little you care for anyone?'

'Jacob,' said a voice so soothing and beautiful that he was immediately stopped in his tracks. 'Jacob!' for that was his name, 'You've been running away for such a long time.'

'How do you know my name?' the businessman said, deeply troubled.

'I try to remember the names of my children,' said the voice, sounding like music from far away, so gentle and lilting, more like a whisper in his ear.

'What was all that about? All those numbers and options!'

'You tell me,' said the voice, but with no hint of criticism. Jacob looked down at his feet, suddenly stirred and ashamed. 'You see all those angels?'

'Yes.'

'You're wondering what they mean?'

'Yes. They're beautiful, but I don't understand it.'

'Neither did your namesake, thousands of years ago. He had spent his whole life manipulating everyone, trying to get to the top at any price. Then he found himself alone, having lost everything, lying in the desert in sheer anguish and despair. You see that stone?'

'Yes.'

'It was a very uncomfortable pillow and he didn't sleep well that night.'

'Did he dream the angels?'

'No, as a matter of fact they were real. I sent them to him, but in the form of a dream so it didn't scare him too much.'

'What was it all about?'

'Well,' said the voice, 'relationships really.'

'Ah,' said Jacob, 'you mean . . .'

'Well,' interrupted the voice, 'I like to consider my angels as the "personal touch". So they came to remind him that even though he was lost in the wide wilderness, he was not alone. He was surrounded by love.'

'The personal touch?'

'Yes. Ring any bells? It's a little rare these days and in some countries it has almost vanished completely.'

There was a long silence as Jacob gazed at his namesake

beneath the throng of angels who were floating up and down a ladder of fire. High above, he could see a brilliant light, but he could not really make out the figure in the trefoil at the very top of the window, only rays of gold and silver, of red and blue and yellow piercing through a dark cloud.

'What did Jacob say to all this?' he asked.

The voice laughed softly. 'Well, he said, "This is an awesome place. I have been standing at the gate of heaven and I didn't know it."'

There was another long silence. 'Is that where I am now?' said Jacob.

'If you would like to be. It's your choice, of course. I could give you four options if you like.'

'No, no!' Jacob cried out loud. 'No!'

'Then would you like me to speak to you in person about your troubles?'

'Yes, please.'

'Very well,' said the voice, 'but this is going to be a long process because we're only just getting acquainted. At least, you're just getting acquainted with me. All I can say for now is that your daughter will be fine. The rest, I can't comment on. That will have to wait.'

'Thank you, thank you,' said Jacob, overwhelmed with happiness at the thought of his daughter.

'I'm sorry I had to lead you into the wilderness so we could make a start on a personal conversation, but that's the way it goes sometimes. I can't promise that you will ever hear my voice again like this, but you will always know my presence.'

Jacob nodded, his eyes filling with tears. Slowly he left the church and the sun was now slipping into the azure sea, filling the whole world with fire.

'Oh, one more thing,' whispered the voice kindly. 'Remember that communion is more important than communication. Togetherness, intimacy, friendship, love. That's how I made the world. I like to keep it personal.'

Cruising Along

Two disciples, now retired, were sitting in deckchairs on a Roman cruise ship. They were sailing in glorious sunlight past an archipelago of islands in the Mediterranean.

'Marvellous,' said Bartholomew. 'What could be better?'

'Yes,' said Thaddaeus, sipping his pina colada. 'This is the life.'

There was a long silence as they gazed at the horizon, where the sun was sinking in the haze.

'I did a few mission trips over there,' mused Bartholomew, waving vaguely in the direction of Cyprus. 'Quite a few people were converted, actually.'

'Really?' said Thaddaeus, helping himself to some delicious canapés being offered by an obliging waiter.

'Oh yes, I was quite an evangelist in my time.'

'I managed to bag a few souls myself,' said Thaddaeus. 'Perhaps not as many as I would have liked, but the persecution was making things rather awkward.'

'Well, that's fair enough,' smiled Bartholomew. 'I think we got out of the race at about the right time.'

'So you got a good deal, then?' said Thaddaeus.

'Oh yes, final salary pension, good pay-off, golden handshake, all that stuff. Actually, I took early retirement at fifty-five.'

'Good Lord!'

'Well, he *was* very good to me!'

They both laughed a lot at this banal religious joke. Bartholomew had a habit of making them.

'Praising the Lord all the way to the bank, then?' Thaddaeus enquired, playing along with the jovial mood.

'I wouldn't take it quite that far,' said Bartholomew, chuckling as he wiped a speck of dust off his sunglasses, 'but I was rather lucky to be one of the last people to be offered early retirement with such excellent benefits.'

'Who offered it to you?'

'I don't know his name – a man in a dark suit. Working for HR, he said. Had unusual feet: cloven, I think.'

'Oh? Well, lucky you.'

'Oh yes, he was all smiles when he came to me and said, "Bartholomew, you've done a tremendous amount for the kingdom, but there is no sense in wearing yourself out, even for such a noble cause."'

'Fair enough.'

'Yes, thoroughly good chap. Of course, I agreed. I was feeling quite tired. That last mission with Paul was ridiculous. Morning, noon and night. We never stopped. Always preaching in the marketplace, in the local forum, debating with philosophers, one town after another – and tent-making to earn our living! I thought that was taking it too far.'

'Oh, it was, it was.'

'He was always trying to make a point. "Mustn't exploit the new converts." He went on about that. "I don't want anyone to think I'm after their money."'

'Well, it was a perfectly reasonable point, but taken to extremes.'

'Yes, he did rather go to extremes.'

'What happened to him?'

'I heard he spent a lot of time in prison in Philippi and in Ephesus and then in Rome. He had a few chances to escape, but didn't take them, which was fairly bizarre.'

'If ever there was anyone who needed to slow down a little, it was Paul.'

'He got this crazy thing about explaining the gospel to the emperor Nero. Wouldn't let go of the idea.'

'Damn fool needed a good holiday.'

'That's what I said to him once, but he just looked at me and laughed for a very long time. Then he said, "Bartholomew, what do you think this gospel is really about? Is the whole idea to make you feel comfortable?"'

'That was a bit rich, a bit "in your face".'

'It was, and I really felt I couldn't work with him after that. I had no intention of driving myself towards a nervous breakdown.'

'Quite right. I can't see how working incredibly hard for the gospel helps anyone.'

There was a long silence after this comment, which hung in the air for a while.

Thaddaeus got out of his deckchair with some difficulty. He had put on a lot of weight since his retirement. He stumbled over to the railing and gazed at the dolphins leaping through the waves. 'This is the life,' he said again.

Bartholomew joined him. He was lean and suntanned and

had kept himself in good shape. 'Beautiful, isn't it? Inspiring, the whole creation. I find myself full of praise.'

'Full of food and wine, too,' said Thaddaeus, belching loudly as he returned to his deckchair.

'You should keep yourself fit, you know. It's important to stay healthy in retirement.'

'Oh?' said Thaddaeus, unconvinced.

'Well, first you want to live a long and happy life.'

'Yes . . .'

'And you have to remember, we're still marked men, you know. The authorities . . . have our names. We're on their list.'

'Ah, yes, so what you're saying is, we need to keep in good form so we can run away from soldiers really fast.'

'Well, not to put too fine a point on it.'

'What did you say happened to Paul?'

'Well, I heard he did his explaining to Emperor Nero thingy and then . . . apparently, he got executed.'

'Damn silly fool.'

'The believers in Rome went on and on about martyrdom and they were quite keen on that. A great many were fed to the lions.'

'Yes, I heard. Well, I'm not really up for that kind of banquet, personally.' Thaddaeus coughed nervously and shook his head. 'All that dreadful business after the fire of Rome!'

'Luckily, I'd retired by then.'

'Got out just in time.'

'But the Roman Christians were quite impressed with Paul's execution. Apparently, he gave them an example to look up to. Boosted morale.'

'Well, maybe, but encouraging your friends by rushing into martyrdom is taking things a little too far.'

'Well, Paul always did.' Bartholomew sat down in his deckchair again, nearly spilling the glass of wine in his hand, but managing to control it expertly. He had had a great deal of practice. 'Praise the Lord,' he said. 'That was a close one. Anyway, what are your plans for the future?'

'Well,' said Thaddaeus, 'the wife and I are downsizing. We're going to sell the villa on Santorini and settle on the south coast of France. Got a smallholding in mind, grow some grapes, enjoy the sunshine, have the grandchildren to stay, but not too often!'

'No need to go to extremes?' joked Bartholomew again.

'No, no,' said Thaddaeus laughing merrily. 'You see, the wife feels that I was away on so many missions, it's really her time now, and you can't argue with that.'

'Not unless you are prepared to face serious persecution.'

'Haha . . . yes. Well, hen-pecking can be the worst form of torture.'

There was another slightly awkward silence, as unease filled the air. Bartholomew gazed seriously out at the horizon. 'Of course, I am deeply aware of what many of my brothers and sisters are facing out there.'

'The ones who haven't retired, you mean?' said Thaddaeus, unhelpfully.

'Well, they should, they should, sooner or later,' said Bartholomew, suddenly very defensive. 'Everyone deserves a rest eventually. It's only right. We've worked very hard for what we've got.'

'Indeed,' said Thaddaeus, who downed a glass of excellent vintage wine that was being offered to him. 'I'll have another of those,' he said hastily, before the waiter could move on.

Twilight was descending slowly and it was a little cool out on deck.

'I suppose we should be heading in for dinner soon,' said Thaddaeus, hopefully.

'Yes . . .' Bartholomew sighed, without moving. 'It would certainly be good to have another slap-up meal.' But he didn't sound entirely convinced.

'I wonder what's on the menu? The wife has probably got one in the cabin. She loves to collect them, you know.'

Bartholomew was clearly lost in thought.

'You seem to be drifting off a little,' said Thaddaeus. 'Anything on your mind?'

'Oddly, I was thinking about Peter.'

'What on earth happened to him?'

'Well, apparently, he was offered early retirement with a very good deal and, hardly surprisingly, he left Rome in a great hurry.'

'Well, things had been getting very hot in Rome, literally.'

'Exactly, and Peter thought, "I've done my bit, I've run the race – well, most of it – and now is the time to make a gentle exit and say a quiet farewell. It's time to enjoy a long and well-earned retirement."'

'Quite right too.'

'Anyway, he was on his way out of Rome, walking down the Via Appia, clutching his financial package and the brochure about his pension rights, when he met a figure on the road.'

'Oh?'

'The figure turned out to be Jesus Christ!'

'Good Lord!'

There was silence and Bartholomew did not exploit this opportunity for another well-worn joke.

'So what happened then?' Thaddaeus was troubled, not least by the fact that Bartholomew was clearly disturbed by this rather sobering reminiscence. 'Did he say anything?'

'Apparently the Lord said, "Where are you going, Peter?" And Peter had some trouble explaining. He realized the Lord had never really talked about "retirement" – not directly anyway. In fact, if we're being honest, not at all. So Peter just said, "There's a lot of danger for the Christians in Rome and many of them are being imprisoned, tortured and killed, and . . ."'

There was another desperately long silence. Thaddaeus looked down at his second glass of wine, which he had not touched.

'Well, he didn't want to say that he was running away or anything. Escaping.'

'Which would be a little unfair for a man who really did – if anyone ever did – deserve to retire.'

'Oh, totally and utterly, yes! The man had earned it a hundred times over but . . .'

Bartholomew gazed at the horizon for a long time. It was scarcely visible now.

'The Lord just looked deep into Peter's eyes and then walked past him. "Where are you going, Lord?" asked Peter. The Lord kept on walking in a very resolute manner. "I'm going to Rome."'

'So what did Peter do?' asked Thaddaeus, aware that the convivial mood of their conversation had now turned very dark. 'Did he, er . . . ?'

'Peter turned round and followed the Lord, back to Rome.'

'Any idea how this turned out?'

'Peter was nailed to a cross.'

'That was unfortunate.'

The lameness of Thaddaeus' response drifted on the night air. The bell for dinner was ringing and his wife was waving from the cabin door.

Bartholomew still gazed into the absolute blackness that had descended over the ocean. A freezing wind was blowing.

'Apparently he asked to be crucified upside down.' Bartholomew's eyes filled with tears. 'He felt he was unworthy to die in the same way as his Lord and Master.'

*   *   *

In the morning, at the very next port, Bartholomew left the cruise ship abruptly, much to the astonishment of Thaddaeus and his wife.

'Where are you going?' shouted Thaddaeus, astonished as his friend walked down the quay, without his luggage, without a penny in his pocket. 'Where are you going?'

Bartholomew did not look back, but called out, 'Rome!'

The Lost Angel

Every year, for more than two thousand winters, the angelic host has gathered for a Christmas reunion in the sky above Bethlehem. The angels fly silently, mysteriously, invisibly from all the dimensions of heaven and from every corner of the universe: the seraphs, dominions, powers, archangels – Raphael, the healing one, Michael, with his sword of judgement and his eyes blazing with the fire of God's holiness, and Gabriel, the beautiful herald of God's love. All gather, in their ranks and orders, down to the tiniest cherub and the most humble servants of this invincible and unseen power. They have congregated above the hills of Bethlehem through the ages to sing a hymn that is heard only in heaven and in the hearts of children who believe at Christmas.

And so, at the end of the year 2019, they were flying from all directions, to the cold sky – above the lorries, the armoured cars, the barbed wire and the brutal concrete. Unobserved, un-remembered by many, the angelic choir began to sing hallelujahs in a world that seemed to have long forgotten the simplicity of the stable; a world deafened by war and hatred, overwhelmed by Christmas greed and chaos and rushing and spending. A world no longer capable, even in Bethlehem, of hearing voices on the still night air, as poor shepherds had once done.

Now it happened that, on the way to this secret celebration for the first time, a very junior angel got lost somewhere near Iceland and, caught on the harsh wind, was blown, tumbling through the clouds, until he found himself hovering uncertainly above a little port on the far north-eastern coast of Scotland. The tiny angel, who had dismally failed his cosmic geography exam, was convinced that he was in Bethlehem. After all, he had seen sheep in the fields and shepherds and cowherds and farmers. He had seen people rushing to and fro on the high street in Wick – for that was where he was – and he thought, *These must be all the people looking for room in the inn.* But what disconcerted the little herald, as he fluttered to and fro in the air, which was filling with snowflakes, was that he was singing 'Glory to God and peace on earth' all alone. There were no other angels, there was no reunion. No great party, which he had been promised. Soon his singing faded and he began to weep, his tears dropping as fine rain blowing over the Island of Stroma and the Pentland Firth. But then, softly, he heard a voice, so beautiful, so loving – a voice far inside. The voice of the Christ-child whispering to him:

'Do not worry, little angel. You have come to a place that is full of praise ringing from the cliffs and the moorlands, a song that rises from the long white beaches and the foaming surf, a music in the rushing water of the burns swelling with melting snow. You have come to a land that is constantly singing my praises. You have also come to a place where there are so many people who are reaching out to me: some who know me, some who think they are far from me, old people who feel lost, young people who are broken-hearted, homes that are grieving, families that are celebrating, children who are laughing and in whose eyes is the hope of the future.

You have come to the far north, which is one of my beloved realms, and the small town of Wick, which is not so unlike Bethlehem. You are in a place where I long to be born in the hearts and souls of the people of Caithness, in the midst of the rush and all the confusion of Christmas. So sing for me, little angel, in the skies. Sing softly, sing of my invitation to all people, so anyone who is seeking will hear my love calling, calling, across the wide open sea.

So the angel sang, filled with joy and pride at being chosen for a solo performance on Christmas night above the skies of Wick. He sang there for a long time, until he was surrounded by lights, by the Northern Lights of God's glorious creation. All the seals swam to the surface of the ocean and sang too, and the porpoises dived and the night-birds called and the fishing boats rattled their moorings in harmony.

And the hearts of men and women and children, who of course did not see or hear the little angel, were nonetheless strangely warmed, brightened by the presence of a love that they had always longed for and sensed was so near them . . . at Christmas, in the little town of Wick.

A Little Girl's
Letter to God

Dear God,

What I want for Christmas is peace on earth. I want my brother to shut up for once. I want him to stop boasting and telling lies and saying he's the most brilliant footballer in the world. Because he isn't. Harry Kane is, but my brother won't admit it. He won't admit anything. He never says he's sorry. What I want for Christmas is for him to be sorry. Dear God, please make my brother nice and kind for Christmas. I am asking this because I know you do miracles. At the same time, can you change my sister? I don't mean just change her. I mean into a nice person. I mean *change* her, like swap her completely for someone else. Please give me a completely new sister for Christmas.

Dear God, what I want for Christmas is peace and happiness. I want my mum to have peace and happiness, but she hasn't got enough money. Dear God, what I want for Christmas is lots of money. I'd give it to my mum. She doesn't buy lottery tickets. She doesn't believe in it. She says it raises her hopes too much and then she feels sad when she doesn't win. Dear God, what I want is for my mum to win the lottery without playing it. I want my mum to be happy. I want the front door mended and a new sofa. I want someone to love my mum. She's very lonely. She says she doesn't like men any more. Dear God, what I want for Christmas is someone to love my mum and not hit her like the last one. She says even Father Christmas can't find her love. Nothing can make her happy again.

Dear God, what I want for Christmas is a clean street and no people smashing windows and no doors kicked in, and I want the old lady in the corner flat to walk outside again and smile and feel safe. Mum says she won't. Not after the last break-in, when they took her pension money.

Dear God, I want a safe world. What I want for Christmas is clean air, a clear sky. I want to see the stars. I can't see them any more. It's too cloudy. It's always cloudy. There's always smoke. If I were a wise man, I wouldn't have seen the star at all. I would have had to stay at home and dream. If I were a shepherd, someone would have stolen all my sheep. I'd have been rushing around all worried, going mad. I'd never have seen the angels.

Dear God, what I want for Christmas is to see an angel. I want an angel here. I want one in my house. Not a spiky gold one on the Christmas tree. An angel for real. I want angels in my bedroom, dear God. I want light all around me.

Dear God, what I want for Christmas is to hold the baby Jesus myself. To rock him and sing to him. I want him with me, then it would be all right. I'd take my mum's hand and show her the baby. I'd show her all the angels. She'd be so happy, she'd be so very happy, she'd cry. Dear God, I want my mum to know that you love her and cry because she's so happy this Christmas.

Dear God, I'm sorry about what I said about my brother and sister. Forget that. I do love them. I'd show them the baby Jesus too. I'd give them at least one quick look at my angels. Well, I'd keep one special one for myself they'd never see. Dear God, I will try to love everybody, I promise. But please make it all better. Please come and see me.

Dear God, what I want for Christmas is you.

Love Sharron

The Ultimate Crash

It all began as a perfectly normal day. People were going to work, shopping, checking texts on their mobile phones, driving their cars. No one would have guessed that the world, as they had known it, was about to end.

There was nothing strange that morning, except perhaps a few alarmist stories in the newspapers and some financial experts muttering about the 2008 financial crash returning with a vengeance. There had been such warnings before, but nothing came of them. It was true that the stock markets had been jittery for several weeks and taken a terrible tumble in the last twenty-four hours, but that was simply 'falling from a great height'. Various financial gurus had smiled to the cameras all the previous evening and reassured the public, 'We are merely levelling out to a familiar position of stability.' They were wrong.

That fateful morning, people pushed their cards into ATMs, punched in their PIN numbers, ordered their cash – and nothing happened. No cards were returned, no money was dispensed and angry customers were left staring at an empty screen flashing on and off.

The violence began with the smashing of the cash machines. People gathered in crowds, wielding crowbars, shouting and swearing, but it was all to no avail. There was no cash to dispense. The banks came next and the first casualties were hapless cashiers who tried, in vain, to explain that they did not have any money, but no one believed them. Soon banks were on fire and employees were wounded and killed. The high street shops were looted, food ran out in the super-markets, the warehouses were ransacked and there were no more deliveries, ever.

Hotels, hospitals, school kitchens, restaurants were ran-sacked. Petrol stations ran dry and the electricity died. No mobile phones, no computers, no television, no radio could function. There was a terrifying silence across the land as all law and order broke down in a matter of weeks, for even the police and the army were desperate to feed their families and soon joined in the burglaries, the ransacking, destruction and murders.

Months turned into years and few survived the dreadful chaos, the famine and disease and tribal violence that gripped the whole world and shook it to the core.

But here and there, eking out a living by the sea or where meagre vegetables could be grown, there were pockets of brave survivors who sheltered in ruined villages, lit fires to keep warm and began to rediscover, in love and friendship, in the presence of nature, a new and radiant meaning to their lives. They could no longer stare at screens all day. They could no longer compare themselves to others who were more beautiful or successful or wealthy than them. They could no longer dazzle their minds with tales of superheroes and block-busting films with brilliant special effects. All they could do was listen to the chattering birds in the dawn and watch the drama of the waves in winter, hurling themselves furiously on to the shore. They could no longer phone friends or text them or worry about blunt or tactless or confusing messages from cyberspace. They could not connect with anything so far away. They could only look their fellow human beings in the eye and commune with them directly.

Despite the desperate harshness of their lives and the bare survival of their bodies, they found that firesides were places of revelation. Instead of downloading stories told by others, they began to tell their own. They began to discover the power of words, of gestures, improvisation and laughter. They began to create little plays beside the fires, and those who had never danced, but merely watched dance competitions on television, began to dance themselves. They began to sing, they began to make up instruments and play them and laugh as they played them.

They began to share their lives and teach their children the art of conversation: how to listen, how to talk, how to think, how to debate, how to give a reasoned answer. And all the people – even these wretched survivors of the most advanced technological age in history that now lay in utter ruins – discovered they could write poetry, however simply, and they could perform it beside the fires, as the flames cast shadows on the rough stone walls, as the sparks leapt up into the darkness of the huge night sky.

The dead plastic in the dead machines, the charred remains of their former lives, were long forgotten. All they could hear was the sound of the seabirds, the cry of the curlews and lapwings and the soaring song of the sky larks in summer, for the birds had thrived and multiplied, and now sang anthems from every shattered wall and broken doorway.

All the people knew, in their very hard and almost brutal lives of survival, was a world in which they didn't complain or long for anything, except to sit round the fires and enjoy their meagre food, a place of safety and warmth where new songs were being sung and paintings were being beautifully created on wood and stone. Young people fell in love, made love, had children, but the new families belonged to the village, the survivors. Indeed, everyone belonged to everyone and there were no individuals intent on 'finding themselves' at the expense of others, because they knew that they survived together or perished alone. There were, of course, arguments, quarrels, accidents, tragedies and heart-breaking bereavements, but even those harsh events gave rise to song and story and memorial and healing.

For these fortunate people, gathering round their fires and eating their meals and looking each other in the eye with confidence, had learnt how to be present. They had learnt how to live purely in the present moment and, in that joyful experience in the context of a desperate world, they had found the one gift they had lost when the 'Pandora's box' of technology had been opened so long ago.

They had found Hope.

The Newcomer

Two angels were standing at the gates of heaven. The senior angel, Wing Commander Luminous, was scanning the horizon with a pair of golden binoculars. His young companion, Flying Officer Cumulus, was pacing backwards and forwards in a state of great excitement. She could hardly contain herself.

'Gosh, Commander! Who do you think it's going to be? Maybe a Roman emperor or a king or famous poet!'

'Possibly,' murmured Luminous thoughtfully, adjusting the focus on his binoculars. 'It's certainly going to be somebody mighty special.'

'Just think,' said Cumulus, flapping her wings joyfully, 'the first person to arrive in paradise after the gates have been thrown open. What a privilege!'

Luminous suddenly lowered his binoculars and stood very still. 'Stand to attention, Flying Officer. Here he comes.'

With that, a figure hurtled through the gates at great speed, tumbling through the air, then dropped suddenly but slowly into the glorious meadow all around them. He lay there for a while, spread-eagled in the flowers and utterly bewildered. He kept shaking his head in disbelief.

The two angels watched in puzzled silence.

Finally, the man staggered upright. He was ill-kempt, un-shaven and had clearly not had a bath for a very long time. He wiped his nose on his sleeve. He then began to look around in sheer amazement.

''E weren't jokin', neither,' he said.

Luminous and Cumulus exchanged anxious glances.

Luminous spoke first. 'I'm sorry, sir?'

The ragged figure continued to look around in awe. ''E weren't jokin' about 'is kingdom an' that!'

Luminous smiled awkwardly. 'I beg your pardon?'

The man walked up to him, a little too close for comfort. 'This is paradise, innit, guv?'

Cumulus laughed nervously. 'Yes.'

The man swept his arm around the glorious scene. 'Terrific, eh?'

Luminous took a step backwards, trying to take control of the situation. 'Er . . . We like it, sir.'

'Like it? Do us a favour! This is fantastic. Look at them trees towerin' like a thousand feet high, wiv every leaf shim-merin' like a gold bar an' all that stuff.'

There was an uneasy pause as Luminous moved over to the heavenly reception desk and shuffled through some papers. He looked up, officiously. 'Do you have any credentials, sir?'

'Wot?' said the man, unhelpfully.

'Papers. Identification. A Certificate of Approval?'

'Got a copy of me death warrant. That any good?'

Luminous was beginning to feel flustered. 'I – I think there's been some mistake.' He closed the file on the desk rather abruptly.

Cumulus stepped forward brightly, in a valiant attempt to lighten the mood. 'What my colleague means is, er, what have you *done* in your life that might give you entrance to . . .'

'Done?' said the man, wheeling on her in the most alarming way. 'You mean, *done in*?'

'I'm sorry?'

'Done in. I mean, I've done in a few people, worked 'em over. Done a bit of blag, y'know, a few good earners, robberies wiv violence, GBH. Yeah, I been around in my time, but never seen no place like this.'

With that, the bizarre new arrival walked off, gazing at the wonders around him with all the fascination of a very small boy. Meanwhile, Luminous took the opportunity to swiftly take Cumulus aside.

'Who is responsible for checking the register of newcomers at the gate?' he whispered urgently. 'Aren't you supposed to be on duty, Flying Officer?'

'With respect, Commander,' Cumulus ruffled her wings in agitation, 'my duty is next millennium.'

Luminous ignored this, waving his hand impatiently. 'Well, even though *technically* the doors are now wide open, there's still got to be somebody doing a spot of eternal vigilance. Now we've got a gatecrasher at the banquet!'

The unsavoury character wandered around happily. 'Look at them flowers like diamonds! I tell yer, if I'd known about this place and seen all this gear, I wouldn't 'ave bothered wiv that job on Pontius Pilate's country residence. No way. I'd 'ave been up 'ere an' ripped this place off. And yet, funny innit . . .' He turned back to the two angels. 'All them lovely things an' that, an' I 'aven't put one in me pocket. I ask yer. Me! Ron the Con! It's a laugh, innit?'

Luminous gulped audibly. 'What did you say your name was?'

'Ron the Con. Get it? Y'know. Tony the Phoney, Bill the Kill.'

Cumulus gasped. 'Did you say Bill the Kill?'

'Yeah, told yer, I done me fair share, then I got pulled in – I got lumbered, didn't I? Well, I ask yer. I didn't know it were Pontius' joint, did I? Course, it were crawlin' wiv Roman filth, weren't it? The whole flippin' Ninth Legion, no less, an' so I got me collar felt.'

'You had what?' Luminous, who spoke a great many languages, was having trouble with this one.

'Are you deaf or summat? I was sussed, weren't I? Wiv the bung in me 'and – all the jewels an' that – wiv me dagger still fresh from the job, drippin' wiv blood all over the shop.'

'You killed someone with your dagger?' Cumulus suddenly became very high-pitched.

The criminal stepped right up to her face and said, 'Well, I didn't tickle 'im under the chin. What's up wiv you lot?'

Luminous pulled Cumulus back to safety. He was now on the edge of panic. 'I'm sorry.' He glanced over his shoulder at the criminal. 'There's been a dreadful administrative error.'

Cumulus looked at the Wing Commander with her deep and dazzling eyes. 'But just suppose, Commander . . .'

'Suppose what?'

'That *we* have made a dreadful error,' she whispered meekly.

Luminous nearly exploded. 'Impossible! Angels do not make errors.'

There was a long pause before Cumulus replied quietly, 'Lucifer made a pretty big one.'

'Now look here! Are you saying . . .'

'I'm just saying that, well, there are things even angels do not understand yet. Maybe . . .'

Luminous rose to his full height, which was quite a lot taller than Cumulus, and gazed down at her severely. 'You're not trying to tell me that all these trumpets and hallelujahs and the splendid apparel and gallivanting around rejoicing and banqueting all over the place are for the benefit of a common CRIMINAL!' He said this far too loudly and was forced to turn round and smile politely at the intruder, who seemed blissfully unaware of the consternation he was causing.

Luminous turned back to Cumulus. 'This is outrageous! It's back to front!' He shook his head. 'I – I'm sorry. I can't believe this. I shall have to go to the top and get official verification.' With that, he flew off abruptly and rather haphazardly, his wing tip nearly brushing against the criminal, who was still exploring the garden with great delight.

Cumulus called after her superior, in sudden desperation, 'But, Commander – don't leave me on my own, he might be dangerous!'

She turned round, hoping to make her own escape, but almost bumped into the ruffian, who was standing right behind her.

'Ah, still here, are you?' she said weakly.

'Yeah,' he said, with that strange mixture of menace and enjoyment. 'Yeah, I thought I'd 'ave a good look round.'

'Oh well, that's nice. Good, umm . . . May I ask who sent you here?'

'Funny you should ask that,' said the criminal. 'I don't know 'is name, actually. I think it was somefin' beginnin' wiv J. He were on the cross next to me.'

Cumulus was shaken, overwhelmed. In one split second, she realized the awesome significance of what he had said. 'You mean – the Lamb of God, the Holy One, the Prince of Peace!'

'No, not any of those,' said the criminal thoughtfully. 'Jesus. That's it! That were the feller's name.'

Cumulus bowed low to the ground, in deepest adoration at the very mention of the sacred name.

''Ere, what's up wiv you? Got stomach cramp or somefin'?'

'O blessed Lord,' said Cumulus, her tears flowing. 'May glory be given to your name!'

'Jesus,' repeated the criminal, savouring the name himself. 'Yeah, that was 'is name and, funny thing, it sounds like music as I says it – Jesus . . . There we were, both dyin', only me for me crimes an' that, caught at it – got me just deserts – but 'im, what 'ad 'e done? Nuffin'. I could see that, couldn't I? Do us a favour. I thought, "Wot's a poor Charlie like that wind up on death row for?"'

He shook his head in amazement as the images came flooding back to him. 'Then I knew 'e were no ordinary geezer. There was somefin' about 'im. Fear. I saw it – not in 'im, no! – in *them*, religious leaders an' that. They were in a right funk, weren't they? Knees knockin'! I saw their game – they were standin' around watchin' to check 'e didn't leap off. I kid you not! Now whoever leapt off a cross, eh? Give us a break!'

Soon, he was completely transported, as the final moments of his whole life came back with all their force. 'Different, 'e were. Talkin' about 'is kingdom. Mumblin', people weepin', holdin' on to 'is feet an' 'im talkin' about comin' into 'is kingdom. I said, "Listen, mate, remember me when you get into that kingdom." Then 'e looked at me. You never seen nothin' like them eyes – lookin', searchin', probin' into me soul. An' then 'e says – straight out, clear as a bell – 'e says, "This day you shall be wiv me in paradise."'

The criminal paused and slowly nodded his head. 'That were the nicest thing anyone 'ad said to me all day. "Paradise? Where's that?" I says. An 'e said nuffin'. 'E smiled. In that agony, 'e smiled. I didn't know where paradise were an' that, but if 'e were gonna be there, I wanted to be in on the act. Know what I mean?'

Cumulus was still lost in wonder, love and praise, with all the criminal's astonishing words ringing in her ears, when Luminous landed suddenly and rather clumsily beside her. He hastily called her to one side.

'This is very embarrassing.'

'I know,' whispered Cumulus, still spellbound.

'We've committed a terrible faux pas!'

'I know. Isn't it wonderful?'

'Wonderful? I've just gone and made a fool of myself with the archangel Gabriel! I said, "There's been a dreadful mistake. This man's a common criminal. He's nobody special at all!" And Gabriel said, "Well, he is now." And I said, "What?"

And he said, "What's your definition of special?" And before I had time to reply, he said that he thought a personal invitation to paradise from the Lord of Life made a person quite special enough, thank you very much. Then all the seraphim laughed their heads off. I tell you, if angels could blush, I would have gone golden.'

Luminous turned to the criminal and bowed very low. 'Your Grace, I really do apologize for any inconvenience my vacillations may have caused.'

The criminal stared at the angel blankly. 'Wot?'

Luminous hastily produced some magnificent robes and began to put these over the astonished criminal's shoulders. 'Here, try these for size.'

''Ere, what's all the flash threads for then, eh?'

'The banquet. You're the guest of honour.'

'Somebody's birfday, is it?'

'Yes, yours. Incredible, isn't it? The last person shall be first, and the first shall be last!'

Cumulus was now helping Luminous dress the criminal in the most glorious apparel. She was laughing and crying as she sang, 'Blessed be the Lord of Hosts!'

Luminous was laughing too as he became overwhelmed with joy. 'Amen. His wisdom is infinite!'

'There is no limit to his mercy!'

'Hallelujah! His love is everlasting!'

'Give thanks to his glorious name!'

Luminous shook his head in sheer wonder. 'In fact, the more hopeless, the better it is. It's a pretty amazing thing, this gospel.'

'Gospel?' said the criminal. 'Wot's that?'

Luminous was stumped for a moment. 'Er . . . well, strictly speaking, it's really justification by faith through . . .'

'Jellification by wot?'

Luminous turned anxiously to Cumulus. 'We're going to have to do something about explaining this to people, you know.'

Cumulus nodded thoughtfully. 'We may well have to re-think our theology.'

'I can't see what zoology's got to do wiv it, mate,' interrupted the criminal. 'I was bein' executed for me crimes an' now I've landed up in paradise. It's fff . . .' He stopped himself in mid-flow, suddenly aware of his sensitive companions. 'It's flippin' marvellous!'

Luminous smiled at this. 'Flippin' marvellous,' he repeated slowly. 'Yes, that's quite a good way of putting it.'

Cumulus laughed merrily. 'Fff . . .' she echoed. 'Flippin' marvellous!'

They all laughed at this as they walked off together to the banquet, shouting in unison, 'Hallelujah! Praise the Lord! It's FFF . . . FLIPPIN' MARVELLOUS!'